PUT A  CRIME IN THE JUKEBOX

---

a Sunny Side UP mystery

MISTY SIMON

PUT ANOTHER CRIME IN THE JUKEBOX
Copyright © 2025 by Misty Simon
Cover design by Daniela Colleo
of www.StunningBookCovers.com

Published by Gemma Halliday Publishing Inc
All Rights Reserved. Except for use in any review, the reproduction or utilization of this work in whole or in part in any form by any electronic, mechanical, or other means, now known or hereafter invented, including xerography, photocopying and recording, or in any information storage and retrieval system is forbidden without the written permission of the publisher, Gemma Halliday.

This is a work of fiction. Names, characters, places, and incidents are either the product of the author's imagination or are used fictitiously, and any resemblance to actual persons, living or dead, business establishments, or events or locales is entirely coincidental.

This book is dedicated to Jason Hagman, who has found many ways to make fun of the way I say words over the years. He didn't help in any way in regard to writing the book, but I promised to shout him out in a book, so here we are.

Acknowledgments

Over the last twenty years of publishing, I have been able to find so many wonderful people in this writing community, especially my Boot Squad who make all things possible. Here's to twenty more years of making each other laugh and cry and swear sometimes over my abysmal knowledge of commas. Love you.

CHAPTER ONE

The jangling of my ringtone sounded just as I approached the back door to the Sunny Side Up, the diner I'd bought with my best friend a little over six months ago. I tried fumbling for my phone in my pocket, but that made me drop my keys, and when I went to grab them, I nailed my elbow on the outside latch for the door.

"Ow! Ow, ow, ow, ow." I finally managed to yank my phone out of my pocket—when had my pants gotten so tight that I couldn't just easily remove it? Was it because I owned an establishment that loved butter as much as it loved sugar? That was a thought to contemplate another time. Right now, the phone was still ringing, and I did not want it to go to voicemail—especially because it could be my old boss Jeb, who I was supposed to be meeting with right now.

"Hello?"

"Jax, yeah, it's Jeb. Look, little missy, I'm not going to be able to—" Whatever he said next was cut off by a bloodcurdling scream.

"What in the world is that?" I asked, a little concerned that I might have to call 9-1-1. After finding a dead body last week, and dealing with the ensuing threats as we'd tried to figure out who the killer was, I was still on edge. What was happening on his little farm?

Instead of a panicked request for help, I got a chuckle as I heard a door slam in the background, cutting off the screaming.

"Jeb?"

"Just Marcus and Brutus having a disagreement." He scoffed. "They're having trouble getting along."

"Should you leave them alone then? It sounds like someone is getting killed there—or at least maimed."

He chuckled again. "Jax, they're alpacas. One stepped on the other. The first one is angry, and the second one is angry that the first one is angry. They'll sort it out. It's not like I can negotiate for them."

His two alpacas. His farm animals were screaming like there was bloody murder happening, and he was laughing? I sighed. At least I hadn't called emergency services. "So I guess you're canceling on me?"

I was bummed because I really wanted him to come over and look at this key we had found in the back of one of the tabletop jukeboxes in the diner my best friend Dani and I had bought from him a little over six months ago. I'd received an anonymous phone call a few days ago, telling me to look for the key, saying it was connected to a murder in the area. We'd solved the murder without identifying the key, but I still wanted to know what it opened. Ever since we'd found it, I'd been trying to get Jeb down here to look it over. He'd refused texted pictures of it, because he hated texting, so I was waiting on him, and now I'd have to wait some more. Ugh.

Jeb lived thirty minutes out from the diner we'd bought from him. At this point, even if he got the beasts to behave and jumped in the car, he'd take forever to arrive because he drove at least five miles under the speed limit. Purposely. He'd explained his reasoning to me one day by saying, "I like to irritate people, and it's not like I'm on a time clock anymore. I've got all the time in the world to get to wherever I happen to want to be."

"Ayup. Can't do it today, girly," he said. "I have to make sure these two don't really try to kill each other or else I'll have to separate them for the sake of the farm and probably my sanity. I'll come in tomorrow to see that key you found in the jukebox during your foray into playing detective."

"Okay," I said grudgingly.

He hung up on me without saying goodbye. I stuck my phone back into my too-tight pocket, which wasn't really as tight as I had thought—now that I wasn't struggling to do three things at once. With a huff, I headed back to my car. There was no need to open up the diner, turn off the alarm, and flip on all the lights if I had nothing else to do here. Everything had already been done when we closed at two this afternoon. Besides that, if I turned the lights on people might think we were open outside of our normal hours when we very definitely were not.

So now I was left with nothing to do in the two hours before the double date I'd agreed to with my best friend Dani and the guy she'd met on the internet.

However, my date wasn't really a date—more of a sidekick I'd picked up during my recent amateur sleuth murder investigation.

Eliot, though, was a tall, really tall, drink of water, and I very much would not mind it if we did start really dating. With dark hair and the greenest eyes, he was very much my type. It didn't hurt at all either that he was over a foot taller than I was and had wide shoulders and a smile that made me feel melty inside. We'd met because he was an ex-cop who worked for my godmother, Hildy, as her head chef. She'd dragged him into helping me look for the murderer of her recently deceased best friend because she wanted justice. We'd gotten through it in one piece, but it had been touch and go there at the end. I was not planning on diving into the amateur thing again if I could help it, though it had been interesting to track clues and interview people in pursuit of getting a killer to confess.

But once had been enough. I preferred much more pedestrian things like making sure the toast was made right and that the eggs were actually sunny side up, if that's what you asked for. Perfectly shaped pancakes were another one of my favorite things, along with divinely mixed milkshakes.

Sleuthing? Not so much. Not again, thanks. Seriously. Finished.

Stella Luna, my frisky Siamese cat, met me as I opened my front door back at home. Lately, she'd taken to trying to escape, so I wedged myself through the door instead of opening it fully to hopefully keep her inside where she belonged. I pushed her back gently with my sneaker and then quickly slammed the door behind me.

"Naughty!" I told her. She just hissed at me and then stalked away to jump onto the back of the couch. Such a diva.

I grabbed my phone out of my pocket, and fortunately, it slid out much more smoothly than last time. Hitting the line for Eliot's phone, I waited through four rings before I considered hanging up. Maybe he was busy ahead of our pseudo-date?

Before I could overthink it too much, Eliot answered. "I didn't get the time wrong, did I?" he asked. "Or did Jeb tell you something?"

"No, Jeb told me nothing. He didn't make it in because his alpacas are acting up."

"Saucy alpacas? Why does that make me want to laugh?" His dry wit didn't have him actually laughing, though.

"You might not be laughing if one of them chose to spit at you in their angst."

"Yeah, true, that wouldn't make me happy." He did chuckle this time, and I swear the sound zipped through the air and down my body in a way that made me tingle all the way to my toes.

Eliot was dangerous—to me—and he seemed very unaware of that fact. I, however, was very aware, and that made me nervous after my last failed relationship even though I was almost giddy about the prospect of starting a new one with a better man.

"So what can I do for you then, Jax?"

"Do you wanna get some ice cream before the movie? Since Jeb canceled on me, I'm left with some extra time and a sharp desire for ice cream."

He hummed for a few seconds, and that did things to me that even his light chuckle hadn't done. Down girl!

"Are you thinking Parker's?"

"Absolutely." And I loved that he knew the best spot for ice cream in town. As I smiled and held in my sigh of joy, my phone started pinging with notification after notification. It'd been malfunctioning for the past few days, and I'd been meaning to replace it, so I just ignored the commotion.

"You want to walk the three blocks, or I can pick you up on my way over. I drive right by your house," he offered.

"It doesn't matter." The pinging of texts intensified. What the heck was going on?

"I'll pick you up then. Give me five."

"Okay," I said, then hung up and inspected my phone to figure out what was on the fritz. But the "malfunction" seemed to be due to a certain friend named Danielle Brighton, my best friend and co-owner of the Sunny Side Up Diner.

Ah, the pre-date jitters. I really should have built that into my schedule. She was probably frantic about what to wear, should she use perfume, would earrings turn him off?

"What's up? Are you nervous about tonight? We can carpool so that if I have to leave, we both have to leave. You know I can totally fake an illness if necessary." I gave her my best cough and ended it with a laugh. But she wasn't laughing, only breathing. "Are you freaking out over this before it even gets started?" Still nothing. "What's going on?"

Her words started cascading out so fast that I had a hard time taking in their meaning. "Didn't you get the alarm alerts? Someone just broke in at the diner! You'd better get down here."

"What? Someone what?" I pushed my light brown hair out of my eyes as Stella Luna jumped down from the top of the sofa and paced back and forth in front of me. I finally stopped her with my hand on her back. She nipped my knuckles, and I shook her off as I dazedly started to repeat myself, but Dani cut me off.

"Broke in, Jax! Someone broke in at the diner! I thought you were here, and I didn't know why you weren't turning the alarm off, and you wouldn't answer your phone. And then the security company called me, and now I'm down here, and I don't know what to make of what the heck just happened!"

"I'll be right there." I hit the end call button and stuck my phone back in my pocket. I was not going to ask what else could go wrong because I was very afraid that the world might just show me.

I didn't even bother with the car, just hightailed it out after locking Stella Luna in the house.

I took my phone out again to cancel my ice cream rendezvous with Eliot. But before I could hit the call button, he motored past me on his way to my house as I stalked along the sidewalk. I heard him jerk his SUV to a halt and then turn around and come up even with me.

"What's up?" he asked, creeping along with his window down.

"Break-in at diner." I kept my eyes forward. I did not want to trip over any part of the sidewalk and add to my troubles.

"Get in. I can get you there faster."

I didn't take my eyes off the view in front of me. "I'm three doors down. Can you please go park in the back and then meet me up front?"

Dani was hanging out the front door, and as soon as she saw me, she started waving at me to hurry up, as if I wasn't already moving as fast as I could. She ducked back into the diner, knowing I'd be following close behind.

The sound of squealing tires had me stopping in my tracks and doing a double take, though.

CHAPTER TWO

Nancy Brighton's car barely came to a rocking stop before she was out the door and stalking toward the diner. To say Dani's relationship with her mom was complicated was akin to saying the Grand Canyon resembled one of our famous Pennsylvania potholes in the road. Accurate but still an understatement.

"Nancy, what can I do for you?" I asked, taking her arm and bringing her up to the sidewalk, simultaneously moving her away from the diner so that no one inside would be able to see her through its big plate-glass window.

"What have you gotten my daughter into?" the woman said with all the indignation of a concerned mother. Not that she really was unless it benefited her.

Hold on a second—I hadn't gotten her into any trouble! I kept those thoughts to myself since I didn't want Dani to peek out and come face-to-face with this dragon of chaos.

"What are you doing here?"

"My daughter is very likely in danger, and I'm here to talk her out of constantly letting you lead her astray. She had so many opportunities in front of her at her previous job until you called and made her drop everything to run back to you."

I was not even going to respond to that. "There's no danger. Everything is fine."

"Then why isn't she answering my texts? Why is she here when she should be at my house helping *me* with all the things I need her to do?"

I took a second to breathe before I answered. "I don't believe anything bad is going on. She was notified that the alarm was going off, so we're meeting here with my father to assess if there's any damage." I hadn't really wanted to tell her about the attempted break-in, but I also didn't want to lie. And since my father had just pulled up and was walking toward us, I couldn't hide the fact that the police had been called.

"Was she already here? Did she do something stupid like try to stop the intruder? That girl, I swear she would be dead if it weren't for me."

I stopped myself before I rolled my eyes and made the situation worse.

Fortunately, my dad, flanked by two other police officers, chose that moment to walk up to me with his hand on his gun. He nodded to me and then looked Nancy over from head to toe, taking in her short, light-brown hair, with its frosted tips, and her turquoise jogging suit.

"Why don't you all go on in and see what, if any, damage there is? I'll be right behind you." He was definitely addressing me and the officers, but he hadn't taken his eyes off Dani's mom the whole time. "Nancy, I'm sure you must be concerned about your daughter's safety, but I can assure you we've got this in hand. There's no reason for you to be here."

Show me how to dismiss someone without actually saying the words…

After scoffing, she seemed to gather herself and assess the situation. Maybe she realized she was not getting in without asking him to move since he had very effectively put himself right in the doorway of the diner.

I was so going to buy him some of his favorite whoopie pies tomorrow and hand-deliver them to his work.

"You let me know what happened, you hear?" she finally said. "I'm not having a very good feeling about our daughters working together if this is the kind of havoc that's going to keep happening."

"I assure you we'll get to the bottom of things."

"And let me know," she reminded him.

He just bobbed his head once and then stood with his arms crossed over his chest. He was not moving until she did, and she knew it.

I could hear her grumbling as she went to her car and got back in. I didn't need to hear her actual words because they'd be the same as always: that Dani was a pain, that she didn't know her place and never did what she was supposed to, and even if she did, she never did it correctly.

As she drove away, I slid past my dad to enter the diner, and he nodded at me. I nodded back. We understood that this visit would not be mentioned to Dani right now. Maybe tomorrow, but not right now.

Stepping onto the black-and-white tiled floor, I took in the red vinyl booths, the way the overhead lights reflected off the chrome on each table's jukebox, and the spotless counters. I loved this place so much, and it made me upset that someone had tried to break in.

I caught sight of Eliot at table three with a flashlight.

"Have you found any damage?" I asked.

"Nope. It doesn't seem like the person was in here long enough to do anything before the alarm went off."

He moved on to the next booth with the little flashlight. Had that been in his car? On his belt? How was he always so ready for just about anything?

I wished I had that same level of readiness when Dani popped up from behind the lunch counter, her eyes filled with tears.

I rushed to her side and gripped her hand in mine. "Hey, what's going on? This isn't that big of a deal. They weren't in here long enough to take anything, so we're good. The till is all here in the safe, right? The silverware is all in the tub, right? We're not out any of our ten million plates, are we?"

That last one got her to chuckle at least. It was a little watery, but it was definitely a chuckle, and that was good. I pulled her in for a hug.

"I feel like things are spinning out of control, and I'm not doing a very good job at anything," she said into my shoulder.

"We're doing fine, and this is not our fault."

"I get that, but it feels like we can't turn around before something else happens."

"Understood, but we'll weather this like we weather everything else. You know what? Let's get things back to rights here, and then we'll spruce ourselves up for our double-date tonight. It can be like the old days. We'll chatter about who we're seeing, and what everyone else will be wearing, and then the songs we really hope they'll play, so we can pick someone to slow dance with. Especially the longer songs."

Another watery chuckle. This one a little stronger, which was a move in the right direction.

I could hear my dad in the back talking to one of his people about any footage we might have on the cameras.

My heart fluttered in my chest. "Uh-oh. Dad is not going to be happy that I have nothing on those tapes, since there are no tapes, because I didn't actually set up the recorder stuff."

"Jax!" Dani said.

"Yeah, well, you can yell at me later. Right now, let's make super sure nothing is gone. Any idea what they might have been trying to find?"

Another shrug from Dani. "Like you said, there would have been no money in the drawer, and nothing else around here would have been worth carting away unless they were looking for a stash of our new placemats."

"I doubt that." I shrugged as I laughed briefly. "Even I wouldn't be looking for our new placemats, and I'm the one who put them together."

Dani nudged me with her elbow. "They're good. Don't sell yourself short."

"Meh, I don't like the picture for the kids to color on the back."

That got a better chuckle. "A plate of eggs, hash browns, and a pancake was perfect for coloring." She wiped under her eyes and blew out a breath. "I'm sorry for being out of control."

"Don't even! We've been going through a lot of stuff lately," I said.

"So how do we get through this without losing our minds?"

Suddenly, "Unchained Melody" came through the speakers on the jukebox down the counter from us, and Dani and I smiled at each other.

"We're stronger than this," she said.

"We sure as heck are," I answered.

"So let's talk with your dad, see what we can do, and then go from there."

"Deal. Give me a second to talk with Eliot."

I looked across the room and found him standing with one of the officers. Even without the uniform, he looked like one of them. Someday I'd get him to tell me all about what had happened to make him leave the force, but for now, I needed to cancel our impromptu ice cream date. He probably had already realized that it was a no-go, but I wanted to say something to him anyway.

I waved to him, and he stepped away from the officer.

"I'm thinking ice cream is off." He had the most adorable

smile, one that had populated my dreams over the last few days.

"Yeah, sorry to call you out and then have to bail on you."

He shrugged those wide shoulders. "It's not a big deal. I'll be seeing you in a little while at the movies anyway. Unless that's off too?"

"No. No, it's not off at all. And this way we'll have more room for expensive theater candy, right?"

"Absolutely. I look forward to it more than I can say."

The way he stroked my cheek as he said those words sent a quiver through me, the good kind. That tingle was still working its way to my toes as I walked back toward Dani.

"Ready in a minute. Let me just check in with my dad," I said, heading into the side room we were currently using for storage.

"Jax, what the heck is going on here?" my dad said. "This is worse than when you were a teenager with your stuff all over the place."

I knew what he was talking about, and I should have thought about that ahead of thinking about the cameras. I closed my eyes for a second as I tried to think of something to say to save myself, but I came up empty.

"Daaaaad…" It sounded so whiny, and I immediately regretted opening my mouth.

"Jaaaaaax…"

"I was going to put everything away." And again, I let those words come out of my mouth without considering what they would sound like to my father.

"I could swear I've heard that for the last twenty-six of your twenty-seven years. That might have been the second thing you ever said, after 'Dad' of course."

Yeah, I knew he was going to say that after I'd tried to say I had put everything away. This wasn't our first time going through this scenario.

"I'm assuming this is where you and Eliot were dismantling the jukeboxes in an effort to find the mystery key?" he asked.

"You would assume correctly."

"And once you found the key, did you then decide to be done, which then led to not coming back to finish the job of putting everything away?"

"I don't know that I'd say it like that exactly. It was more that we were so jubilant to find the key and wanted to immediately begin finding out what the key belonged to, so we moved right along to the next task of asking Jeb if he knew what it might go to." I sounded a little more petulant than I wanted, but that was what he got when I felt on the defensive. It was like I was being thrown back to my adolescent years.

"Without completing and putting away the last task."

"You're killing me."

"I'm not trying to kill you," he said, smiling because he knew he very much was. "I just want to make sure I have the lay of the land so that we can see if anything was actually stolen or if the perpetrator was intimidated with your alarm system, that appears to lack cameras."

"Nothing is missing," I confirmed.

"As long as you're sure." My dad raised an eyebrow.

I nodded and raised both back at him. "I'm told the person wasn't in here for very long, and nothing is disturbed."

"How could you tell in this room?" He gestured around, and I knew what he was talking about. The two tables to the left were covered with seven jukeboxes in various stages of dismantling. "You might want to put cleaning this up and returning all the jukeboxes to working order on your list of things to do."

"It's there."

"Maybe move it up." He smiled, and I laughed.

"Yes, Dad."

"Okay, enough of that. I had someone check with the people next door, who do happen to have cameras, and are actually using them, and it looks like the person popped the lock, but as soon as the alarm started blaring, they hightailed it out as fast as they'd come in, empty-handed."

"If nothing was taken, and they ran right back out the door, are we clear to go then?"

"Yep, have fun on your non-date double date tonight. I like Eliot, by the way. Not that you asked, but I thought I'd offer it anyway."

"Thanks, I think I might too." In reality, though, we'd only known each other a few days, so I wasn't sure what might happen next.

* * *

In the end, the getting-ready process was a blast. It was as if we were both deliberately putting the attempted break-in behind us and gearing up for better things to come. We probably used more hairspray than necessary, but in the end, we were presentable and in much better moods than just an hour before.

"So how vetted is this dating site?" I asked, looking in the mirror in my bathroom and trying to decide if I should make wings on my eyeliner or just leave it as is.

"It's not really a dating site." Dani turned her head back and forth to see the whole picture of her face. Her dark hair was pulled back with a clip and her brown eyes sparkled with a new shadow she was trying out. "We ended up following each other through social media because we liked the same post, and it turned out we have some mutual friends." She touched the lipstick to her upper lip one more time and then nodded at herself in the mirror.

"And these are reputable friends? Not just people you used to work with or someone you think you've met but really only know online?"

"Yes, Jax. Give me some credit."

"You can have all the credit," I said, patting my pixie cut and making sure those wings at my eyes were killer. "I'm just looking for where it came from."

"We're good, and if his pictures aren't twenty years old, he's very cute."

Well, that was something at least, and if he was twenty years older and looked more like a walrus, we'd deal with that when we got there.

Shooting Eliot a text to let him know we were heading out, I made sure Dani had buckled her seatbelt and then got on the road. She stared out the window the whole time, so I left her to her thoughts in case that was what she needed right now. After I found a parking spot, we grabbed our belongings and set out for the ticket booth.

"You ready for this?" I asked.

Dani nodded and stuck her thumb nail in her mouth.

"No nail-biting. It's going to be fine. It's just a movie, and if he tries to hold your hand and you're not ready, we can switch seats. Promise."

"So I can sit next to Eliot and cuddle with him?"

I snorted. "Yeah, no, we're not going that far."

We'd been so deep in conversation that I hadn't realized there was a commotion up ahead until I tuned back into our surroundings.

Two females were screaming at each other, surrounded by a crowd of aghast onlookers. Was it kids? Were there two high-schoolers deciding one had looked at her boyfriend wrong, so they were going to brawl on the sidewalk out in front of the movie theater?

I tried looking over people's heads to catch a glimpse of the inside ring, but there were too many tall people in my way.

"I wonder what's going on?" Dani said.

Somebody yelled "fight," and the ring shifted enough for me to see that one of the people in the center was *very* familiar to me.

CHAPTER THREE

"Backstabber," Dani's mom yelled as she lashed out her hand and struck the woman opposite her. Just a slap, but both hands were windmilling, and the other woman started doing the same thing. Since they weren't landing many hits, the screaming and slapping would have been comical—if it had been on the big screen in the building behind them and not involving Nancy. Standing out on the sidewalk in front of the movies? Not so much.

I tried to scoot Dani behind me so that she wouldn't have to deal with the embarrassing scene, but she was not having any of it.

"Mother!" She stepped into the fray, shoving Nancy back from the other woman, who smacked Dani's back a few times before she realized that someone had stepped in. When she made contact the last time, she stopped mid-smack and stepped back, horrified.

And that was when I realized the other woman was June Foster, a loan officer down at the bank. What on earth had happened that Dani's mom and June were going at each other like a couple of elementary school kids squabbling over who had called first dibs on the only playground swing?

Ultimately, it didn't matter. I stepped in with my back to Dani's and stood face-to-face with June. Her horrified expression turned into teary eyes and a huge sigh.

"If you want to tell me what's going on, I'm willing to listen," I offered.

She shook her head and backed off, turning to walk into the theater, and bypassing anyone who tried to check in with her, including a trio of women that she turned her head away from as she walked past them.

She wasn't marching along with her head held high, but when she glanced back before the door closed on her, she just shook her head and continued on.

I finally turned to find Dani restraining her mother and

trying to talk her down from whatever ego-bruising insult must have started the fight.

"Mom, it is not worth it. Whatever happened and whatever was said, it's not worth getting into trouble. I don't want Jax's dad to have to come out and give you a citation for fighting."

"And he would. I know he would." Nancy bristled and bunched her hands into fists. "He's not a very nice man either. You should have seen the way he looked down on me today when I was just trying to help my daughter, but he wouldn't even let me in the diner. He stood there like a giant, looking down his nose while not letting me in. It was horrible."

Dang it! I had hoped her earlier visit to the diner would not come up tonight and that I could avoid talking about it with Dani at least until tomorrow.

Dani looked at me over her mom's bowed head. I mouthed an apology. Dani briefly shut her eyes then sighed.

"What movie were you here to see?" Dani asked. "Do you have a ticket we can turn in?"

I winced because if she was going to be at the same movie as us then we were going to have to sit with her. That would definitely make for an even more awkward first double-date. Ugh.

Nancy frowned, pulling her silvering eyebrows together. "I don't have tickets. I saw June standing over here when I was heading to the grocery store, and I had a question. But as soon as I asked, she started yelling at me. I was only defending myself. And then she started hitting me. She'd better be glad I didn't pull out my lucky sticker!" Before my very eyes, Nancy opened her purse to flash a pink utility knife with a bedazzled handle.

Dani gasped and glanced wildly around the area. "Put that away! And what were you fighting about?"

I noticed Dani didn't mention that Nancy had actually been the one to hit first. I also knew trying to get Nancy to admit that would only prolong things and make them worse, so I let it pass.

"That's none of your business."

"Mom…"

"None of your business!" She stamped her foot and then stalked off.

Dani started going after her, but I pulled her back by her elbow. Eliot had just arrived in his SUV, and the guy whose picture I'd studied, to make sure he didn't look like a felon, was coming from another side of the parking lot. He was also a tall glass of yum—light hair, more slender build than Eliot, and a smile for every person he walked past. I would almost bet he had a sparkle in his eye.

I breathed deep then launched into my false, but absolutely needed, hype voice. "Your date is here, and he is adorable. Your mom is going to sulk whether you follow her or not. I would stay right where you are if I were you. Think about it."

She closed her eyes for a few seconds and took a deep breath. "You're right. This is my night, and I'm not letting her ruin it."

She followed my lead when I turned her toward the other side of the parking lot. Eliot had caught up with the internet date, and they must have found something to talk about since they were currently laughing together and then high-fived.

"Is that good or bad?" Dani asked, her eyes following the tall duo as they made their way toward us.

"Hopefully good, but we can totally reserve judgment as needed."

Eliot jumped up onto the curb and made a beeline for me first. We stared at each other for a second before he smiled and then stuck his hands in his pockets and rocked back on his heels. I wouldn't have minded a hug, but it looked like I wasn't getting one unless I initiated it. I pondered the idea but ultimately chickened out and didn't try. We hadn't really talked about that kiss we'd shared a few days ago, and it hadn't happened again, so I wasn't sure where we stood on public displays of affection. Now wasn't the time to ask, so I stayed where I was and simply smiled at him.

"Ian?" Dani asked.

"Yep. Your pictures are wrong," he said, and I braced myself. "They totally do not do you justice."

Oh, nice save, and the way Dani smiled and sighed at the same time made me really, really hope he would be the gem Dani deserved.

"Thanks." She shifted from side to side and tucked her dark hair behind her ear.

"Do you two know each other?" I asked Eliot.

"We go to the same gym. I met him a few weeks ago when I was lifting weights. He helped me to correct my stance."

Considering I'd never lifted a weight in my life, unless you counted Stella Luna, I could only infer what he meant. But at least it was confirmation he had seen Ian around and trusted him to help with his training.

"So we're seeing the movie at eight." I glanced at my phone. "Which is right now." I herded the two very handsome men and one dazzled woman to the front door. We still needed to get the tickets from the booth and had to move now if we wanted to be seated before the movie started.

Which unfortunately meant no popcorn for me. On the bright side, though, I had stashed some candy in my purse, so I wouldn't be completely bereft of snacks. Ian said he had to make a quick stop in the restroom and would meet us inside.

The theater wasn't packed, which was nice. I saw June, the woman Nancy had been fighting with, sitting up at the back of the theater. The bright white of her shirt was stark in the well-lit theater. With her arms draped over the backs of the two seats on either side of her, she looked like she had staked out the row and was not open to anyone sitting near her.

Ian showed up as we were finally making our choice of seats. We filed into the row about halfway up the stairs, and I could hear Dani giggling like a schoolgirl as I saw her blush.

The lights dimmed and the ads started rolling just as we took our seats. Eliot chose the outside seat, and I sat next to him, with Dani right down from me and Ian beside her. For all the people who had been outside for the fight, there were very few people in this theater with us. Really it was only two other couples on opposite sides of the theater, a gaggle of female gigglers calling for everyone to sit down near the top, and June two rows above them.

"I wish I had popcorn." I hadn't planned on saying it, but then I couldn't stop myself. The disappointment was strong, and the trailers usually ran for about twenty minutes anyway. I should have just stopped to get it before we'd come in.

"Butter? Lots of butter, right? I'm not putting salt on it," Eliot said.

I squeezed his hand. "And a soda?"

"Cola. Got it. I'll be back."

"Did you want anything?" I heard Ian quietly ask Dani. "I don't mind going out to get something for you."

"No, that's okay. We're settled. Unless you want something? I'm okay with whatever," Dani said.

He chuckled as he laced his fingers through hers. And she held her breath. She was in deep already, and I wanted that for her.

Not wanting to invite myself into their conversation, I tapped my toes on the floor while I waited for Eliot to come back.

Once he returned with a completely saturated bucket of popcorn that probably assaulted his very essence as a chef, we settled in for two hours of adventure, dramedy, and witty banter. We laughed, we gasped, and I got to cling to Eliot's arm during the truly twisty ending that was both satisfying and yet bewildering. The gaggle of gigglers in the theater caused a ruckus during one steamy part of the movie, and one of them screamed in laughter, which was followed by them all shooshing her.

We stayed through the credits, even as the other two couples got up to exit the theater, chattering amongst themselves. The giggling gaggle, including the screaming laugher, left next. I recognized a few of them from around town.

I could never leave before the lights came up, just in case the director was going to throw some extra awesome onto the end. Ian, Dani, and Eliot didn't move either after I asked them to please stay. June must have thought something more was going to happen too, since I hadn't seen her walk down the stairs and out of the theater. There was nothing, though, and eventually, the house lights went up.

As the ushers came in with their brooms and trash cans, I stood up and watched a female usher mount the stairs heading towards June. I glanced back up at the upper seats to see if June was the only person left in the theater with us. She hadn't moved, like at all, since we'd first sat down. Her arms were still draped over the backs of the two seats on either side of her. Was her circulation just that phenomenal or were her arms going to be dead when she finally let them drop down to her sides?

I couldn't see the usher's face, but she seemed to be asking June to move along, and June was ignoring her.

Was she deliberately being obstinate? Maybe she was miffed at the whole world after that slap fight with Nancy. That thought flew out of my mind when the usher nudged her, and June rolled forward and fell to the floor. As her body twisted, I saw a large bloom of red on the back of her shirt.

And that's when the other woman screamed bloody murder much like Jeb's alpacas earlier that day. Except, this time, it was because that was exactly what had happened.

Uh-oh.

CHAPTER FOUR

───────

Eliot was already on his cell phone calling the police as he and Ian ran up the stairs to June to see what had happened and help calm the usher. I stayed at our seats with Dani. My brain couldn't let go of the question of whether June had been dead since we first walked into the theater…

Dani grabbed my arm right above my elbow, jarring me.
"This is horrible. Who would do this?"
"I have no idea, but I'm sure my dad will figure it out." I was just thankful I wasn't by myself this time when a dead body was found.

My thoughts were interrupted again by my dad showing up at the bottom of the stairs. He glanced our way then walked past us to join Ian and Eliot above.

Normally seeing my dad two times in a day would be a good thing. But recently, seeing him twice in a day involved interacting with him in the capacity of his job. And I didn't like that as much since it meant trouble.

"What should we do?" Dani asked.
Glancing up at the three men, I tried to sort out what might be the best way to handle things and came up short. "I think we should just wait here. I don't want to get in the way, and we don't know any more info than the guys about what exactly happened. Let's just stay at our seats until my dad comes to talk to us."

"Jax," my dad said sharply from five rows away.
Had he been calling my name while I was talking with Dani? I guess I hadn't heard him with all the thinking I'd been doing. "Dad."
He pointed to his badge.
I sighed. "Detective Tapman."
He nodded his head. "Any idea what happened here?"
"Not really, other than I'm thinking that June Foster is dead." I probably should have been less dry when I said that, and from the

look on my father's face, he was not amused. He was not alone. Our town used to be so laid back. Gossipy, yes, and snarky, yes. But not murder-y.

"I don't know anything more either, Detective Tapman. I don't even know how long she's been dead," Dani said, a certain level of horror in her voice that I completely understood. There was a dead body in the room with us. Anyone would be horrified.

"Did either of you see anything at all?" Dad, *Detective Tapman*—excuse me, asked.

"No, we came in right before the ads and then watched the movie," I said as Dani just shook her head.

He sighed. "All right, well, if you think of anything let me know. We'll deal with whatever happens as it happens."

"You know where to find us if you need us." I scooted out of our aisle and took Dani with me.

"Yes, I do. Be safe. I don't like how things have unfolded over the last few hours."

"Right there with you, *Detective*." He leaned in to hug Dani and then me. I gave him an extra squeeze before we left the theater.

After we exited into the hallway, I turned to Dani "Let's wait for the guys by the soda machine."

Chatter was incessant at the concession stand, and employees were talking over each other to share what they knew and ask about what they didn't. They seemed to know nothing more than we did and had the exact same questions. I guided Dani toward the butter dispenser instead of the soda machine because I thought it would be more out of the way.

A moment later, Dani gasped next to me, clutching my arm so hard I thought it might leave marks. "What are we going to do about my mom?" Dani whispered.

In all the commotion, I hadn't even thought about that. Some former amateur sleuth I was. "It's going to be okay. My dad is good at what he does."

I knew that to be true. On the other hand, I wasn't so sure that Dani's mom wasn't about to get grilled for the fight she'd started earlier and the death of her opponent. We needed to tell my dad before he left, but I didn't want to bust back into the theater and interrupt him while he was working.

"What am I going to do if your dad thinks she did it? What if she did it?" She drew in a quick breath. "Of course, she didn't do it.

My mom might be a lot of unsavory things, but she's not a killer." She turned pleading eyes to me, and I, of course, nodded at her to show that I believed what she was saying.

I really didn't think her mom would kill someone. Definitely not with a knife in the back…

My thought trailed off because suddenly I very much remembered Nancy not being afraid to flash her pink-handled utility knife and calling June a backstabber right before we'd broken up the fight. Oh, my word…

"We're going to have to tell my dad," I said, leaning back against the counter. "I wish my brain had been working in the theater. I just couldn't focus on anything but June being dead. We have to tell him about the fight and the knife, even if we don't think she did it, if we want the right person caught for this."

She huffed out a breath and then lifted her gaze to mine. "I know. I know he needs all the information, but I really wish we didn't have to say anything."

"Yeah, I wish we didn't have anything to say."

"Yeah, well, me too." She sighed again, and we both were lost in our own thoughts for a few minutes as the employees started leaving their clusters and got back to work closing the place down. We might have to go stand out front at some point, but since the air was cool on this fall evening, I wasn't leaving until I was told to.

My dad emerged from the hallway to the left and headed our way. I was happy to not have to chase him down. "Dad, we weren't thinking about everything earlier in the theater. We have some new info for you."

Thankfully, he didn't correct me on his name this time. He just blew out a breath. "That's why I was hoping you were still here. Dani, I heard your mom got into an altercation with the victim before the movie. Do you know what it was about?"

"No, I'm sorry. She wouldn't tell me. I could ask her again?" Her words sounded hopeful at the end there, like she was asking permission to do the questioning instead of him.

"You're more than welcome to do that, but I'll also have to talk with her to make sure we have all the correct information to solve this."

"Of course." She dipped her chin and looked at the floor.

"Hey," he said softly, placing a hand on her drooped shoulder. "I don't think your mom did this. I just want to see if she has any insight into what happened and what the fight was about so that I can rule her out."

"I understand. I just know she's going to be devastated."

"Because June died?" Dad asked.

"No, because you'll be questioning her, and she'll be furious. She's already mad about you not letting her into the diner after the burglary, so if you question her, just brace yourself for her to be really angry."

"So noted." He rubbed his chin for a second, which had always meant he was thinking and trying to figure out how to phrase his next thought. "What if you tell her that I've given you permission to collect information at the diner like you did last time? That way she thinks you're helping, but you stay out of harm's way?"

After what Dani had said about her worries with her mom, I'd just been considering that same idea. Apparently, this apple didn't fall far from the tree. We saw lots of people from town at the diner, and last time we'd done a ton of information collecting just by listening to the gossip over eggs and coffee. Maybe this time it would work too. And I would do anything to help Dani, even if that meant redonning my sleuthing hat to look into this murder to clear her mother's name.

"That would probably work best," Dani said, looking very relieved.

"The only thing I'm going to ask then is that you be very careful. I don't want either of you to get hurt. If you find yourself in a bad situation, don't get in too far. Call me at the first sign of trouble and try to keep your sleuthing to the collecting gossip angle. I don't want a repeat of last week's drama if we can help it. Okay?"

This time we both nodded. With our conversation pretty much over, his gaze rose to look beyond us, and I wondered if now was the time to tell him about the knife Dani's mom had, before he left to his next task.

Dani cleared her throat and beat me to it. "She had what she called a sticker in her purse. It was a little pink utility knife with a decorative handle. I don't think she did it, and I don't think she used the knife, but I wanted you to know so that you know everything we do, even if it looks bad."

He took his notepad out and wrote something down. "Anything else?"

"No," Dani said. "She told us the fight was none of our business and then left. I would swear she got in her car and drove off right after that."

He tapped his pen on the notebook. "I know this is not going to be easy for you, Dani. I will do everything in my power to find the real murderer. I promise."

Biting her lip, she nodded, and then he took off. If he pulled Nancy in as a suspect, I knew I would be asking tons of questions, at least at the diner.

Turning, I gripped Dani's hands. "Are you okay?" I asked.

"I'm not sure." She sighed and flicked her gaze back out to the window in front of her. "Did your dad say anything that should make me not okay?"

"He's going to find the person who did this." I hadn't really answered her question, but it was the best I could do.

Out on the sidewalk, Ian leaned against the exterior wall by himself, looking around.

"How'd he get out there?" I asked, but then I saw the local EMTs come around the corner with a covered stretcher. The theater had fire exits for each screening room, and he'd probably used that instead of coming back through the lobby.

As we stepped through the double doors, Dani waved to him, and he came trotting over, putting his arm around her shoulders.

"I know this is a weird first date," Dani said, her gaze remaining glued to the sidewalk in front of her. "I'm sure it's not quite how you would have wanted to start out."

I watched him stare down at the top of her head, and I waited.

"It's been interesting, to say the least."

She scoffed. "Yeah, interesting. I'm sorry."

"No need to apologize." He used just his fingertip to lift her chin and looked into her upturned face. "I'd be game for a do-over if you are."

Biting her lip, she nodded.

"Did you know the woman who was killed?" he asked. "I was an MP during my military stint, and it's never easy seeing a dead body. It's even worse if you knew them personally. I'm sorry you had to go through that."

"Thank you." She nearly whispered the words, and I wasn't sure what to do. I was almost positive that she was more concerned she might know the killer, but I certainly didn't want to bring that up in front of Ian. Maybe it was better to just leave it all alone and call it a night.

She huffed out a breath. "You didn't answer my question, Jax. Did your dad say anything that would make you think he's going to look at my mother as the killer?"

I shot Ian a quick glance, but his face registered nothing other than curiosity. "Um, no. You heard everything I did. He gave us the all clear to collect any info we hear and share it with him. We just have to be careful."

"We will."

"Tomorrow we can rope the diner staff into helping out again."

"Okay…" She seemed to be half in and half out of our conversation. What was she thinking?

"You can turn me down if you want, but I have some experience with this kind of stuff too if you don't mind me helping," Ian said.

"I hate to ask," she said.

"You're not asking. I'm offering." He smiled and cupped Dani's cheek. I could have sworn she was about to melt into that touch, and I wouldn't have blamed her in the least.

I liked this one. He was adorable, and his smile could light up a whole town even in the middle of a tragedy.

"Let's call it a night then, and we'll move on poking around tomorrow. Ian, you can come in for breakfast if you want, and we'll start a game plan."

At that moment, Eliot strode out the glass doors, and all thoughts of Ian's adorableness flew right out of my head. He might be cute, but Eliot was a whole other bushel of wow.

Down, girl. I had things to do. Like ask a favor.

"Eliot, I think we're going to have to ask around—"

"Already on it, and there are a few things we need to discuss. Not here, though. I think I have good information, but I am going to need to verify it before I believe it. Think Stella Luna might object to company? I can cook up something from whatever's in your refrigerator while I talk."

"But I wanted to…" I trailed off because I realized the parking lot was deserted, and I'd lost the opportunity to snag any of the employees to see if they knew anything they wanted to share. I hoped I would remember most of the people who had been here tonight so that I could look them up or press them if they came into the diner. It was as good a plan as any at this point.

"Ian, I don't know if you are okay with coming to my house…" I trailed off, not wanting to make decisions for him but not wanting him to feel pressured either.

He dazzled with that smile again, just a kick up of one half of his mouth this time. Still very effective. "I know Eliot from the gym, and if he's comfortable with you, I'm willing to take a chance. Besides if you get frisky, I'll just sic him on you."

He laughed, and I was left wishing for a different kind of friskiness, courtesy of Eliot.

Clearing my throat, I looked to Dani. "Up to you, honey. You want to go home, or you want to have snacks prepared by a five-star chef while we discuss whatever the amazing Eliot has managed to suss out over the course of a handful of minutes?"

Finally, she looked up at me. "Your house. I'm going to need answers, no matter what they are."

So we headed back to my house. Upon entry, I did everything I could to keep Stella Luna from attacking Eliot, but she insistently laid claim to his lap with no apparent intention of ever getting up again—which meant he was not making five-star chef things in my kitchen. As a result, I ended up rummaging through the cabinets and getting drinks for everyone.

I put out some dip and chips and then placed what I lovingly called my snackle box on the glass coffee tabletop. It was filled with all the things people would normally put on a charcuterie board but in the little cubbies of a tackle box. Once that was placed, I sorted out the drinks. Yes, I had carried everything out in one shot. I might primarily be the overseer and not the deliverer at the diner now, but that didn't mean I couldn't still deliver with the best of them.

Eliot had taken the time I'd been in the kitchen to get Ian up to speed on our previous shenanigans that had turned into a real-life catch-the-killer moment. I could vaguely hear him over the crinkle of opening bags from the pantry and the fizzle of drinks being poured.

I figured if he'd left anything out, Dani would fill in the blanks. She still looked a little lost but had at least taken up a spot next to Ian instead of curling into the one easy chair all by herself.

"So we have a new mystery on our hands, but my dad yielded enough to give me permission to listen to what's being gossiped about and report back, as long as we stayed safe." I leaned against the back of the couch, not ready to sit just yet.

"Did that help last time?" Ian asked, sliding a spoon into the dip then shaking some chips out onto a paper plate. He handed it to

Dani before grabbing another for himself.

Dani's eyes softened as she laid a hand on his wrist with a smile. "Thanks."

"Sure thing." He winked at her, and even I almost swooned.

Eliot cleared his throat while he shot me a look that had edges of *what are you looking at* to it.

"Back to what we're here to do." Eliot cleared his throat again.

"You mean beyond having snacks and figuring out who killed June?" I perused my choices from the snackle box and then chose to shove an entire handful of almonds into my mouth.

He just shook his head at me and grinned. "Yes, beyond snacking, unless you want me to leave and take all my information with me."

"Hey now." Or that's what I was trying to say, but I started choking on the almonds I almost inhaled. Eliot was up in a flash, thumping me on the back.

I staggered forward and gripped the island counter. I had managed to swallow the nuts right before he jumped into action and took a deep breath right after. I laughed, and Eliot stopped his jerky movements, turning me around to face him.

"Your timing could be better," he said, using the flat of his palm to rub my back instead of smacking it to save me.

"Your moves are divine," I returned as I enjoyed the sensation of him rubbing soft circles between my shoulder blades before sitting down, feeling a slight glow at his heroism and humor. It was time to get into the real business, though. "So tell us what you found out, oh great questioner."

"Who knows Mildred Case?"

Dani and I immediately looked at each other with our eyes wide.

"Everyone knows Mildred," I said. "Emphasis on the 'dread' part of her name."

CHAPTER FIVE

Eliot chuckled at my statement just as Dani groaned. It was no joke that nearly everyone knew Mildred and also dreaded her. She'd been around town for many, many years, both in the chamber of commerce and at the bank where most locals had gone for loans over the years. She also liked to participate in as many community events as possible even though she was never a smiling face in the crowd. She just wanted to make sure everyone was following the rules and doing things her way. But we all put up with her because she had been around for a long time and was from one of the founding families of our town.

Seven months ago, Dani and I had been sitting in her office for an hour, handing over document after document, hoping she'd approve the loan we needed to buy the diner from Jeb.

He had said we could maybe do a rent-to-own kind of agreement, but I had not wanted to be beholden to anyone but a bank for the funds needed to start things up. I also hadn't wanted to mix business with friendship outside of ownership with Dani. I was thankful Mildred had eventually approved the loan, but I did not want to have to deal with her again. Ever.

"What does she have to do with this?" I asked.

"She seemed very sincere and concerned," Eliot said, shrugging his shoulders. "She was there to see some three-hour movie that started an hour before ours, a tearjerker from her description. According to her, she wasn't surprised June had been killed because there's been some unrest around the banking and financial decisions June has been making recently. She was, however, surprised that yet another murder happened so quickly in this small town."

"Yeah, well she and June were quite the pair. I'm not saying we shouldn't find out what she knows, but I am going to caution you about believing anything that comes out of her mouth. She likes to make things bigger than they really are."

Eliot frowned at me. "Why do I get the feeling that you're going to want me to take her on by myself?"

I smiled at him. "Because you're just that astute, my dear Eliot."

That got an eye roll, but I wasn't kidding. Eliot was more than welcome to interview her until she talked his ear off.

There was every possibility she wouldn't talk to me anyway, and I told him as much.

He harrumphed. "Well, someone's going to have to do it, so I guess I'm taking one for the team here? Especially since we weren't able to talk to any of the theater employees. If nothing else, it could give us a jumping-off point to verify the information with a more reliable source."

Spoken like a true former police officer and detective. "Precisely. And in all honesty, I bet it will go far better if you're the one asking the questions without interference from me or Dani. Maybe she likes you, and if she does, then it's best to have you talk with her. You'd be one of three people in the world she does like. Of course, one of the other people is herself, and the third has been dead for twenty years, but you have at that."

He groaned, but he did make a note on his phone and then gestured for me to continue. Okay then.

"What else do we know? I feel like this murder is totally out of left field. Was it someone just taking advantage of the timing and opportunity to kill her, or was it actually planned out? June might not have been loved by everyone, including your mom, Dani, but what could have happened recently that would make someone think they should kill her? And why at the movie theater? Was it something that just happened or was it revenge served cold years later?" My mind again went back to the knife Dani's mom had flashed from her purse, and my stomach sank. What if it really had been her? We were going to have to look into that if only to rule her out. But what if it only made it look more like she was the actual killer?

"I keep saying it can't be my mom, but I saw that knife in her purse too, and I can't ignore that she can get extremely nasty if she's crossed. But murder? I don't see her being able to actually do that."

"Valid point," Ian said. I'd almost forgotten he was there since he hadn't said a word up until now. "The thing is, some people can be on a tipping point for years. It can take only one small incident to send them straight over the edge. But if you don't think that could be your mom, and you want to make sure we can prove it is someone other than her, then we need suspects, credible suspects, other than her. I'd be happy to help."

He had his own valid points, and we might need all the help we could get depending on what we found. The last murder investigation we'd been a part of had shown me that people I thought I knew were not always who they said they were. That had rocked my boat on trusting new people too. But I felt like Ian was one of the good ones.

"Okay then, let's start with the people who might have issues with June." I tapped my finger to my bottom lip but remembered I had put lipstick on and stopped. Then I almost laughed aloud at myself. I'd shoveled popcorn and candy in my mouth like it was going out of style before nearly choking on a mouthful of almonds. My lipstick was long gone.

"We could have the diner employees keep an ear out for gossip again." Dani folded and refolded a napkin in her lap. "And believe me when I say that June was not exactly a pleasure to deal with in any event. Before we bought the diner, I used to work with her in the banking industry, and while I dreaded Mildred, I would avoid June like the plague. We should look into who else June dealt with outside of work to see if there was a recent issue."

"Hmmm, well, since Eliot is already going to talk to Mildred, he could ask her first."

"I'll add it to my list," Eliot grumbled.

"Wonderful, and good luck getting out without some scarring."

Eliot groaned again "Is she really that bad?"

Dani and I both nodded. I placed my hand on top of his. "She's just a little bit difficult to deal with, but I'm sure you'll do great."

"Should we make a master list?" Dani asked, rising from the sofa to pace. "Do we need a murder board? I can run to the store and get one."

I glanced at the clock on the wall behind her and chuckled. "I don't think anywhere is open at this time of night that would have poster board for us to start making pathways on. Why don't we reconvene tomorrow to see what we have?"

Dani sank back into the chair, and I understood her need for action. When I had thought I might be pulled in as a suspect for the previous murder, I wanted to go full-bore twenty-four hours a day to find out who had actually done it. No rest for those proving you weren't the wicked. No slack given so that I could make sure I was not pulled in for something I did not do.

But on the other hand, what more could we accomplish tonight with no real new information and nothing to move on other than guesses?

"Well, before we go, why don't you tell us what you—"

Dani's phone started chiming like someone was aggressively checking out their groceries.

"What the heck is that?"

Dani shrugged as she bobbled her phone from the coffee table. Because of my position, I couldn't see what was coming across the screen when she opened it, but I watched her face go from curiosity to downright anger to then irritation.

It had to be her mom.

"So what is Nancy bringing to the table?" I asked.

"Well, to start with, she wants to know if I am looking for whoever actually did this since she can't trust the police, and apparently, we owe her. 'We' as in you and me. And if we did it for the last murder, we should have no trouble doing it for this one."

I rolled my eyes because what else was I supposed to do? Of course she'd put it like that instead of asking if her daughter would possibly help by looking into things and then providing said info to the police. Beyond that, she should be incredibly thankful that her daughter's best friend was the offspring of a cop and, therefore, could help if she was so inclined. But that would never come out of Nancy's mouth—or her fingers, as the case may be.

"Then she started listing names. I'm assuming they're all people she thinks we should look into?"

Why did I have the feeling we were not going to be able to get away with keeping Nancy out of things and that she was going to act like the biggest Karen manager in the world?

Off the table I grabbed a pad of paper and the pen I'd laid there last week when I'd messed up my Sudoku. I'd actually wanted to chuck it across the room but made myself stop and breathe before gently laying it down on the glass surface. "Hit me with it."

"You're going to want more paper than that."

She wasn't kidding since the dings were still coming in. How was Nancy so quick to type?

"Choir, ex-husband, inheritance, high school rivals. She's listed every single person in her graduating class…Oh come on! I'm not even going to…" She sighed and put the phone down. "She thinks the woman at the supermarket checkout, whom she had to correct about change the other day, could be one of the suspects. I'm not doing that. The first four could make some sense, but I'm not chasing after the woman who jogs by on Tuesdays and Thursdays that my mother honks at every morning and makes her jump just because she can."

"Is that the kind of stuff we're going to have to tell her we looked into, but it didn't pan out?" Eliot said.

All eyes were on Dani. I watched the anger come back and start boiling in her bloodstream. Then move up her face in a flush that could not be mistaken for shyness.

"No, we're just going to look into people who might have an actual motive. She can text all she wants but I'm not chasing a thousand people down."

Thank goodness for that. "Well, let's ask the staff tomorrow to keep an ear out for anything sordid about Nancy or June, and then we'll go from there. No harm and no foul in at least keeping our ears to the ground," I said.

"Okay." She blew out a breath then typed a reply that took about a second to send. Good for her. After tucking the phone into her pocket, she folded her hands on her lap. "What are the chances you have any of that tea I love?"

"Funny enough, I just made a run for it today and would be happy to steep some for you."

She nodded. "Please."

"Anyone else?" I asked as I got up from my place on the couch.

"Nah, I'd better go and get to sleep. Early day tomorrow. But if you need any help, just ask. Seriously," Ian said with his strong chin jutted out just a little and his light hair slightly mussed. "I might not know everyone in town like you all do, but that doesn't mean I can't be of help. It's funny how very few people pay attention to you when they think you've moved on to your next task."

We'd experienced that too, so I didn't have that hard of a time imagining it.

I waved to him as Dani walked him out to the front door. She went all the way outside with him and let the door close behind her, which meant she wasn't getting back in unless I unlocked the door from this side. Rookie.

But I figured it was going to take her a few minutes to say goodbye, so I turned to Eliot. "You sure you're up for this?" I asked. "It's not like you don't have another full-time job, and I know Hildy can be demanding of your time."

He hummed low in his throat for a second and then nodded. "Yes. There's something going on here, and as much as I want to just cook, I can't let this go. My brain keeps circling the *how* and the *why* and the *why now*. I might not *have* to do this, but I want to help Dani too. Besides, your dad asked me if I'd give him an assist if I come across anything that might help."

I wanted to be a little salty about the fact that my dad warned me away and yet invited Eliot in, but it did make sense. "You know, he likes you." I said it casually, but I really did love that my dad had said not only that he liked Eliot but that he liked Eliot for me. I liked Eliot for me too. Problem was, I was nervous that, even if he liked me back, I might end up treating him like a rebound.

"I appreciate that he does, but I think it's more that I made him a steak the other night he absolutely loved. He wouldn't stop telling Hildy how much he loved it. Apparently, no one is allowed to make his steaks except me from now on. Even if he's grilling out back, he wants me to come over and do the grilling for him—but just for him."

"I bet my aunt loved that, not only for her but for her posh restaurant. That's quite an endorsement for your kitchen and her reputation in general. My dad knows a lot of people in town, and if he says you're the best, that could be even better for her business." I chuckled, and that got a half smile out of him.

"Anyway, I like Dani, and even if I don't know her mother, I feel like I can help. Call it intuition. Call it gut instinct. Whatever it is, I feel like I have to look into this, and it's only upped by the fact that I can see your friend is hurting, and she's my friend now too."

What a freaking cinnamon roll! He was tough on the outside and super gooey and adorable on the inside. My heart fluttered, and I told it to stop. Like now. How about *now*?

Fortunately, Dani took that moment to rattle the door handle and then bang on the door when I didn't get there in a split second.

"I guess I should go get that," I said, shrugging.

He chuckled for real this time. "Probably, before she throws a brick through your side window and crawls in."

That got me moving. I almost sprinted when she pounded on the door while peeking in the window at the side of my door.

"Took you long enough," she said as she strolled in. Her skin was flushed, but I wasn't sure if that was because she'd been kissed soundly or if she'd worn herself out by pounding on my door as if I wouldn't have let her back in without her making a scene.

And then, before the door fully closed behind her, someone else came darting into my house.

CHAPTER SIX

———

"What are you doing here? You need to be out investigating things! You need to be figuring out who would do this to me!"

I swear if Nancy was going to keep showing up where she was very much not wanted, or needed, then I was going to go into hiding. And once I was in hiding, I would not come out until she was gone—whether in jail because she really had done it or exonerated by someone 'fessing up.

"Mom, what are you doing here?" Dani stood back from her mother with her arms crossed over her chest and her hip cocked out as if in challenge.

"Watching you kiss some man I don't know and messing around when you should be doing the serious work I told you to do. You're lucky I got here after he left, but if I see him again, I will tell him you are unavailable."

Dani's whole body bristled, and I braced myself for whatever came next. "No, you will not. And nothing was done to you. June was killed tonight. Tell me you're not so selfish as to not see there are bad things happening to people around here and that the world does not revolve around you."

Nancy's whole face flushed red, like Dani's had been a minute ago but for very different reasons.

"You're ungrateful," Dani's mother said, pulling her cardigan tight around her middle. "You've always been ungrateful. I can't count on you for anything." And then she started sobbing and collapsed onto my couch. Of course she did.

Dani turned her back to us and placed a call on her phone. "I need you to come pick her up. I can't do this."

Knowing she'd called her stepdad and that he would be here soon, I opened my front door to the night air just so that he could collect Nancy the moment he arrived instead of having to knock on the door. It might only cut off three seconds, but I wanted this done as soon as humanly possible. Letting in a little chill was worth it.

And then time passed at an excruciatingly slow crawl as the three of us stood awkwardly transfixed by the scene that was Dani's mom and her crocodile tears. Finally, Herbert showed up at the door.

"I can drive myself," Nancy said to her husband as soon as he came through the door. She didn't look at him. She just rose and left, and then there was a quiet in my house as we all kind of avoided looking at each other.

How was this going to go now? I was prepared for almost anything.

Dani started laughing.

Well, maybe except for that.

"Did you hear me? Oh my word. It was like something came over me, and I just thought *no, you do not get to do this to me,* and I actually said the words out loud instead of locking them behind my super-clenched teeth. It's like a liberation." And she laughed again.

Okay, this was going to have to be played carefully...

"Good job." Oops, that kind of came out like a question rather than a statement of encouragement.

She just laughed more and flopped onto the couch then pulled a pillow to her stomach and hugged it.

Okay then.

"So, um, are we still looking into the murder?" I asked because I wouldn't have been overly surprised if she decided to let her mom swing in the wind on her own after this, at least until she got over being furious.

"Oh, we're going to look into it, all right," Dani stated adamantly. "But not for her. For me. So that I can know what's happening and also never feel like I have to do anything for her again."

I glanced at Eliot to see how he was taking things. He looked vaguely concerned, but you couldn't always tell with him.

I jerked my head toward the kitchen so that we could have a quick meeting.

He followed along behind me and then immediately started rummaging in my cabinets.

"It's a little late for whatever you're going to create out of nothing."

He hummed as he opened cabinet after cabinet. He eventually turned to me with his half smile and a twinkle in his green eyes. "Just scoping out for the next time," he said.

And my heart fluttered. Next time…

Stella Luna chose that moment to come over and leap onto the counter between us. I'd become accustomed to her territorial behavior toward Eliot, so I just gave her the side-eye.

"Before you say anything about me backing out, or being uncomfortable with Nancy's behavior, let me tell you what I think."

"Okay." I drew the word out.

"It's no different than what I said when Dani was outside with Ian. If I can help Dani get this figured out before anyone else gets hurt, then I'm in."

"Same."

"Then we're in agreement and don't have to go back and forth with the should we shouldn't we. Excellent." A full smile spread across his face, and I was glad I was already leaning on the counter for support.

My always sassy Stella Luna hissed at me and took a swipe, but Eliot quickly grabbed her up and calmly brought her to his chest. She looked up at him like he had all the treats in the world at his fingertips.

Same, girl. Same.

"Okay." I cleared my throat of whatever was clogging it—jealousy? I sure as heck hoped not. She was a pet, and I was not. "Okay, so we do the most we can to help out Dani, but if things get dicey, we just keep low to the ground. I don't want to get almost taken out like last time, you hear me?"

"Loud and clear." He nuzzled the back of Stella Luna's neck before bending over to place her back on the kitchen floor. He was so tall, so very much taller than my five and a half feet. My cat did a few figure eights around his ankles and then sauntered off, but not before she stared me down for a good five seconds. Brat.

"So what's our next step?"

"I have ideas." Dani came sailing into the kitchen with determination on her face and a chip on her shoulder that was probably forty pounds of sass. That I could deal with.

"I agree that we might not be able to talk to everyone involved right away," she continued. "And I know your dad wants us to be careful, and I get that. So tomorrow we work and get the Spy Spindle out."

"Spy Spindle! Oh, my goodness! What an awesome name for the ticket spike! Yes!" I would defend my overuse of exclamation points on this to my death. Last week, we'd taken one of the diner's metal spikes we normally used to collect paid checks throughout the day and turned it instead into a collection device for any information or gossip our servers or bus people heard throughout the day that might lead to finding the murderer. With her quick and wonderful naming of this tool, my cheeky girl was back, and I loved that for her. "Fabulous! We should use the sticker-maker to put its name on the metal base and make it official."

She smirked. "Yes, I've been sitting out there trying to come up with something catchy to call it because it took my mind off of everything else that seems to be going out of control. Anyway, we get the Spy Spindle out, we do the work at the diner during the day and collect any info we can while serving the best food in town. You know people are going to be talking about the murder like they did before. Then tomorrow afternoon we go to your mom and see what she remembers from back in the day."

Oh man, my mom. I'd had to talk to her about back in the day last time too. She had not exactly been happy about me dragging things up from the past, but she'd done it. For me. And I had no doubt she would do it again for Dani. I just wished I didn't have to ask.

I sighed and frowned, trying to think of how we'd approach her.

"Don't even try that," Dani said. "We went through all kinds of stuff for your Aunt Hildy in that last crime because one of our lanyards was used as the murder weapon. We're doing this."

"Come on, you know me better than that. I wasn't trying to signal that I wasn't going to do it. I just know it brings up some things she doesn't like to remember."

"We can be as gentle as possible, but there's no one else we can ask that we'll know isn't hiding something."

"You're totally right. Tomorrow it is."

She hugged me tight then gathered her things and left. And so it was just me and Eliot, who was leaning against the stove with his arms and his ankles crossed, not cooking anything. Why not?

Right! Because it was after eleven, and he'd said he was peeking around to make plans for next time, which I hoped would be soon.

Oy, it was after eleven, though. That fact finally registered and gave me pause. If I had any prayer of getting up in the morning to run our diner, I needed to go to bed right now and definitely not with a full stomach of delicious food made from whatever I had on hand.

"Thank you for wanting to do this," I said. I could get used to seeing him in my kitchen.

"Of course. I told you I wanted to do this way before she put her proverbial foot down, and you know it." Stella Luna chose that moment to leap onto the counter and then into Eliot's arms.

He caught her effortlessly and smiled, and I smiled back at him then rested my hands on the counter. "There's no stopping you, is there?"

At that he really did laugh, and Stella Luna jumped out of his arms at the way his chest shook. She flicked him a look over her shoulder as she also flicked her tail and went off to parts unknown to show her displeasure.

With his arms empty, I was very tempted to step in to fill the void, but with the way he'd avoided touching me earlier, I wasn't sure if that would be welcome.

Besides, we had a mystery to solve, and I did not need to add my own desires into the mix of what could already be seriously convoluted.

Right. With that decision, I went to the fridge to get myself a glass of my favorite sweet tea and then take myself to bed after seeing Eliot out.

But as I went to pass him, he reached out and pulled me into his broad chest. My heart sped up, and with my cheek resting right at his heart level, I could feel it thudding under his sweater.

"I wasn't sure how you felt about public displays of affection, since we hadn't really talked about it before we kissed. So I wanted to wait until we were alone to see if that was the beginning of something, or if it really was just an in-the-moment thing that you might not want to repeat. Just a flash in the pan because of your relief things were over in the investigation."

Have you ever had your cheek resting against someone's broad chest and felt every word rumble against your face and down through your entire body? Highly recommend. Twelve out of ten.

"I wasn't sure if you felt the same about the kiss. It's not like I asked you if it was even okay to kiss you last time," I said.

He loosely set his arms around me and rested his hands on my hips. Held but not caged. Delicate and yet spicy in its own way. Yowza!

"For future reference, you do not have to ask me ever." He squeezed my hips. "I will always be open to...well, anything really, except another box of that macaroni and cheese you had last time."

I rested my forehead on his breastbone and laughed. "So noted." I looked up, way up, into his smiling eyes. "So what do we do next, former detective?"

He smiled down at me and locked his hands behind my back, giving me another little squeeze before settling his lips over mine and taking that heart flutter straight into the realm of hummingbird activity. His lips were soft as I sank into his arms and the kiss. Absolutely heavenly. I could stay here forever. But after another minute, he gave me one last brush of his lips and then went about letting me go and setting me back a step.

"Now we say good night," he said, placing one more kiss on my cheek. "And then we get ready to do some serious sleuthing tomorrow. I'm not going to tell you that you have to follow my lead, but I would like to be included in discussions or decisions you make *before* they happen this time, if possible. It goes much easier if I at least know what you have planned."

"Can do." I put my hands behind my back to where he'd touched me, still feeling his lingering warmth on my lips. Lovely.

"And tomorrow I work in the evening at the restaurant, so if you want to drop by the kitchen and give me a debriefing, I'm sure Hildy would be okay with the pit stop. That way you don't actually have to eat there, just pop in."

"I do prefer the food you make here instead of having to be all the way across the room and out of sight."

"I prefer it too." He moved away from the counter and paced backward toward the door. "You're done at two-thirty?"

"Usually." I followed him two steps away, and it was like we were doing a dance. I desperately did not want the song to ever end.

"I'll come by then before I have to report in at four. That way we can look at the Spy Spindle—and yes, that is a crafty name for it, and then we can decide what the best angle for your conversation with your mom might be. You can come by my work afterward and let me know what direction you think we should go in from there."

Seeing him twice in one day again? I could definitely do that. "Sounds good."

He was at the door now. He grabbed his coat off the rack in the foyer, and Stella Luna emerged to twine around his ankles one more time before he left.

After opening the door, he stepped through. I kept my two-step difference, but he closed the gap by lifting my hand from my side and slowly pulling me forward, and then he planted another kiss on me that curled my toes again.

"Jax Tapman, your mother taught you better manners than that." The words were yelled from a passing car. It was my aunt, if I wasn't mistaken, and I was sure I was going to have to hear ribbing about my supposed untoward show of affection from my mother tomorrow.

But that would be tomorrow, and if I was already going to get in trouble, then I was going to make it worth it.

CHAPTER SEVEN

I didn't keep Eliot for long in the doorway because I didn't want to tempt myself too much into wanting to bring him back in where it was warmer and far more comfortable than standing half-in, half-out of the house.

Leaning against the door frame, I watched as he got into his SUV and waved to me one more time before taking off down the street toward his house—or whatever he lived in, since I'd never been there. That gave me pause, but I shook it off because a lot had happened over the last week.

I really had to get to bed. Morning was going to come faster than I wanted, and I had to be ready for it. No doubt it would be a day filled with so much more than just making sure we had enough coffee and that the home fries were crisp without being burned.

As I went through my normal routine of brushing my teeth and washing my face, I ran over what had happened today—from the lack of info from Jeb, to the break-in, to the slap fight, and then the murder at the theater. And then my mind flitted to that knife Nancy had stashed in her purse.

For Dani's sake more than anything, I didn't want Nancy to be the culprit. But no matter how much I told Dani that I knew her mom hadn't done it, I didn't know if I was one hundred percent certain I was right. I knew I'd never tell Dani my thoughts, but I was going to keep an open mind about whatever information we found. If it did turn out to be Nancy, I'd be there for Dani to help her pull the pieces of her life back together. We'd done it more than once for each other, and I'd do it again and again.

Stella Luna followed me around the house as I shut off lights and set the coffee maker for o-dark-thirty. I loved the diner, but I sure wished people didn't expect it to be open at six every morning. Dani and I had talked about making the opening hours a little later, but the first time we'd tried, we had a line at the front door at one past six and then people knocking on the glass starting at two after the hour. It hadn't been worth it. I'd finally opened the door at ten after the hour, and even though I'd just turned on the griddle and the coffee pot had just started to drip, the patrons didn't care because they were in their booths, starting the tabletop jukeboxes with their favorite selections, and that was enough for them. We never opened past six again, and some customers would have been happier if we started at five. No way no how was I giving in to that demand, though.

Stella Luna jumped up onto the bathroom counter as I changed into my pajamas, and when I went to throw my clothes into the hamper, she dove for the arcing shirt as it sailed toward the basket. She caught it before it hit the plastic and then ran away with it. Probably to nest. I would have liked to have done the same thing since I could smell Eliot on it, and that smell was divine. But I would have other opportunities, so I let her go and got myself ready for bed.

Normally, I read to fall asleep, but this time I was asleep before my head hit the pillow fully.

I was restless throughout the night, alternating between wonderful dreams of boat rides with Eliot in a gondola for some reason and a bunch of dead people staring at me, wondering when it was going to be their turn for me to solve their issues so that they could move on. I would not be touching the latter with a ten-foot pole, and the gondola rides probably had to do with me fiending for more of the delicious pasta Eliot had made that one night at my house. Though, maybe, I really just needed a vacation from all this strife and drama.

What happened to my dream of just serving up coffee and unburnt toast to the masses every morning and then hanging with my cat at night, reading and relaxing? Poof! Gone, at least for the moment.

By the time I actually woke up, it was later than I had intended. That realization sent me into a frenzy of rushing around and doing my very best to not trip over Stella Luna, who seemed to have decided that wherever I was, there she, too, needed to be.

I knew it was useless to try to keep her out of my bedroom, or the bathroom for that matter, so I just did my best not to fall flat on my face when she darted between my legs.

Eventually, she went back to her nest of clothes that smelled like Eliot, and I left the house without her trying to dart out the door.

Maybe I needed to get more clothes that smelled like him if it would keep her calm. It would keep me calmer too, if I was being honest.

Thankfully, it was a short distance to the diner. I'd bought my house years before I'd been able to buy the diner, anticipating that someday Dani and I would achieve our high school dream of owning the establishment and making it a success. When I saw the line at the door waiting for us to unlock and start seating, I paused. This was the dream come true. Walking up to the door, I could hear the talk in line about what had happened yesterday, how it was yet one more mystery and had anyone heard anything. I acknowledged that the town murders weren't actually bad for business even though that felt rough to think, much less say. On the other hand, I had always tried to make the most of any situation.

"We'll be open in about ten minutes," I said as I went down the line to enter the diner.

Janice Forrester looked at her watch and then back at me. "Eight minutes."

"Right. Yes, I'll get on that." I hustled a little faster and hoped with all my might that Dani was already in there with Terri and the crew, firing up the griddle and whisking the eggs.

Instead, I walked around the building, through the back door, and into a very specific kind of chaos.

"Look, if you expect us to not only do our job but also keep our ear out for all gossip, then I feel like every slip we put on your Spy Spindle should count for something. What's the point if we're being expected to do so much more but get nothing for it?" That was from Jacob, a newish hire.

"You get the satisfaction of knowing you helped find a killer and bring them to justice." I shoved my purse into a locker and then put my hands on my hips.

Terri laughed. "There is that, and we know it, but you are asking for a lot with all this stuff."

"No doubt, and I understand," Dani said before I could jump in. "But this time I would really appreciate it too. My mom might be one of the suspects. It's important to me to clear her name, and I'd really appreciate your help doing that."

There was some low-key grumbling but also a few nods and a few whispers that I wished I could have caught. The noise level was too low to do anything but watch their lips move and wish I could read them.

"I get it, and I understand we're asking for a lot. Tell you what." I glanced over at Dani and knew she wouldn't object, so I continued without checking with her first. "Put your initials on the corner of each slip you put on the Spy Spindle. For anything that pans out and for the sheer amount of info we manage to get, I promise there will be some kind of prize. Maybe a gift certificate to a favorite store or a dinner over at the Poplarsville Inn." Surely, my Aunt Hildy would give me a discount if I asked very nicely.

There was some chatter, and then the staff turned to me and nodded. Good enough.

"Now, we have four minutes to open and a line of people very impatiently waiting out there to come in and drop all their theories and ideas and stories that might lead to a killer. So keep your ears sharp and your serving skills even sharper."

More nodding and then everyone scurried off to do their thing.

Dani turned to me with a smile, and her head tilted to the side. "Thank you. I really appreciate that."

"Ha! You might not when you see how much of our money is going to go to Aunt Hildy if people find really good info and put it on the spindle over and over again. It could end up leading to a valid suspect that turns into a caught killer but also a hefty prize bill for us. I don't know that we can write that off on our taxes."

"It would be worth it," she said then left the back room to go open the doors.

I sure hoped she was right.

The morning flew by, and that spindle was stacked in the first few hours. Words and theories were flying through the air, and the information just kept coming. June had not been liked by many, actually, which I had known but not really to the extent I was hearing now. It was as if everyone had simply been waiting for her to pass before airing their real feelings and grievances about the woman, who I hadn't thought was a big part of daily life around here. Apparently, I was very wrong. What else was I wrong about?

I didn't have much time to think about it, though, because I was off and running, bussing tables, pouring coffee, and being told that no one wanted me back on toast detail. One mishap with burning the toast by accidentally putting it down twice and suddenly I was unable to cook anything. Ungrateful wretches. But they were hanging out and tipping well today, so I wasn't going to say anything out loud.

Terri motioned me over to the grill, and someone groaned behind me.

"Pat Fredericks, no one wants to hear your complaints," I said and then went to Terri to see what she needed.

"We're going to run out of eggs," she whispered, and my heart stopped because it wasn't even ten in the morning yet. We had hours and hours and omelets and over-easies galore to make. What the heck had happened to our egg supply?

I didn't have time to guess and would check the inventory and the last order we'd received after we were closed. Right now, I needed eggs, and I needed them immediately.

"I'll go see what I can do."

"You'd better just go to the grocery store. We don't have time to wait for Jeb to decide to get down here." Terri clinked her spatula onto the grill and then waved her hand for me to be gone. Nice.

I went to snag Dani as she stood with a tray full of dirty dishes next to the table populated by the giggling gaggle who'd been in our theater last night. They'd left before June had been discovered, but they all seemed to know about it now as they talked incessantly about how it could have been one of them dead in their seat. Jess squealed at something her cousin said, then glanced my way and lowered her eyes. Kimmie followed the direction of her gaze and smiled at me while flipping me a little wave.

"Can you believe we were in the theater with a killer?" Kimmie said and her other cousin, Bianca, was the one squealing this time. I didn't know the other three women at the table, but I was pretty sure they were the same group from last night. I'd called them girls, but, really, they were close to my age, which put them in the woman category.

"It's wild," I said. "Did any of you see anything that could help the police?"

They all shared a look and then shook their heads.

"We've been talking about going to the police station though and giving statements to the cops." Kimmie turned her coffee cup around in a circle on the table in front of her. "We might not know anything or have seen anything, but if we can help, of course we'd want to do that. It's so scary to think that someone went up during a movie and plunged a knife into that poor woman's back and no one even knew it. How long had she been sitting there dead? Did you hear her scream or anything? The movie was so loud—who knows when it actually happened!"

"Exactly," her cousin Jess said. "I mean, it could have been any time. Do you think they snuck up behind her? The seats are low, but they'd have had to creep along the row right above her to do it and then sneak back out. How did everyone in there miss that?"

All very valid questions and I made a mental note to ask my dad if they'd been able to figure out when exactly June had been killed.

But for right now, I needed to get Dani away from the table so that I could tell her about our egg crisis. "I'm sure he'd appreciate any and all info." I topped Kimmie's cup off while I was there and then motioned for Dani to follow me away from the table.

"We're running out of eggs," I said quietly to Dani once we were out of earshot of their table.

"What?" she yelled. "That can't be possible!"

Note to self, remember who you were dealing with when it came to these kinds of things.

"Shh. It's not the end of the world. I just wanted to let you know that I'm going to run out and get some. Don't make a scene, and no one will know."

"Right. Right. Right. Everything just seems so off-kilter right now. Sorry."

"We're good, and no worries. I'll be right back." I dropped the coffee carafe off before walking into the back room.

Taking off my apron, I set it on the counter and grabbed my purse and keys from the locker. It might be a short distance to the diner from my house, but I still drove in case I didn't feel like walking home after being on my feet for eight to ten hours, depending on the kind of day we were having.

Starting up my car, I considered where to go. Technically, I could race over to Jeb's and back. Per my mental count, we had at least an hour's worth of eggs left as long as no one came in and decided that today was the day they were going to try to out-egg everyone else and order scrambled eggs by the dozen. But I couldn't count on that. So instead, I went to the local grocery store and grabbed a few cartons, and then I grabbed a few more, just in case, because if I didn't, someone was absolutely going to come in and order them all in one fell swoop.

When I got back to my car, I saw something jammed under one of my windshield wipers. I wanted to grab it and see what it was right away, but I also had my arms filled with egg cartons, and the last thing I'd want to do was drop them all in the parking lot.

I opened the back door of my car, transferred the eggs in, and then shut the door, now feeling hesitant about what I'd find on the windshield. With the previous murder, I had found nasty messages on my and other people's cars, and I'd also received more than one letter warning me to stay away from investigating anything, along with other messages that gave me info I didn't know what to do with.

Well, the answer wasn't going to come to me while I stood there and contemplated. I snapped the windshield wiper up and grabbed the object, which turned out to be another note as I had feared. What would this one say? I figured I wouldn't know until I opened it.

Back Off. No One Wants You To Get Hurt.
Well, that was clear enough.

CHAPTER EIGHT

———

I stared at the note, looking for any hints as to the sender. Was there something significant about the way the person wrote the letters with a green pen, capitalizing the first letter of each word? Something about the thin notebook paper they'd used? After about fifteen seconds, it occurred to me that whoever had left this was probably still nearby. I whipped my head up to look around the parking lot, but there appeared to be no one out here with me. Plenty of cars but no people.

I crushed the note in my hand because, here was the thing—I did not need to be told what to do or not do. While I appreciated that no one wanted me to get hurt, I could not stress enough that I was capable of making my own decisions.

The nerve!

But the note still scared me even if it wasn't exactly a threat. I looked around the parking lot again and saw no one lurking around.

I got in my car, smoothed the note out on the front seat, and then drove back to the diner. At this point, I was contemplating not telling anyone about this note just yet. I didn't want to worry Dani or my dad before I had a chance to do some thinking.

For right now, I needed to get back with the eggs. The rest of the day would just have to unfold as I worked through what came next. We were meeting with Eliot after work to find out if we had any solid information and decide what to do with it if we did. Then we'd head to my mom's and see what she had to say about the June and Nancy debacle and if it would give us any leads.

Because that was really what I needed, reasons why Nancy might have been on someone's hit list to frame for June's murder, but currently, we had nothing. I didn't like having nothing.

By the time I'd worked through all of that, I'd made it back to the diner and was collecting the eggs from the back seat when someone knocked on the roof of my car. I nearly jumped out of my skin until I saw it was Eliot, and then I groaned because, in the few seconds it'd taken me to recover myself, he'd seen the note on the front seat and was not only pointing at it but also frowning. Was it wrong that I wanted to kiss away the crease between his dark eyebrows?

Not if I kept it to myself and didn't actually act on it…

I opened the other back door then handed him the eggs because he might as well be of some use if he was going to force me to explain the note before I was ready.

"Take a second before you get yourself all worked up. I was going to tell you about this when I saw you this afternoon. I just got it off my windshield at the grocery store."

"The grocery store? Had you been planning to go there?" He held on to the eggs but also looked over my shoulder to see the note better.

"No, it was last minute. Somehow, we were almost out of eggs even though I know we just got some in a few days ago. But Terri said we were down to the last flat. So I had to go to the store because I couldn't wait for Jeb to get down here. Can you please take them in? I don't want to have to tell people they can't have their over-easy."

"Oh yes, that would be the bitter end of the world."

I gave him the side-eye, because he knew it would be for my customers, and just kept walking toward the back door. I was positive he'd follow. What else was he going to do with six cartons of eggs?

I held the door for him and then trooped in behind him, wanting to get this day done and over with so that we could move on to the other important things, like finding out if anyone had any solid leads on who would have wanted June dead, and why now?

I placed four of the egg cartons in the refrigerator in the back and took the other two up to Terri. She was cracking her very last egg into a hole in a piece of bread to make an egg-in-a-hole. Her whole face relaxed into a smile when she saw me. Normally, she rolled her eyes, so this was a positive turn of events. Maybe I should let supplies run down more often.

"Please tell me you got more than that! I just got an order for seven omelets, four sets of scrambled eggs, and five Eggs Benedict."

"What the heck! Who's here, the marching band?" It was a valid question. A few weeks ago, they'd been practicing in the football field and all decided to crash here afterward. I would swear on my best spatula that I went through four loaves of bread and two flats of eggs in minutes.

"No, it's the choir over at St. Pete's. They wanted to have some sort of personal wake for June this morning, and since she hated to eat here, they all decided this was the best place to show their respect for the soprano they hated to deal with."

"Oh, ow. And yikes on top of that."

"Yeah, check in with Dani when you see her. They've been insinuating that they'd like to thank her mom for taking care of things, and it's not going over well for her."

My bristles and my hackles immediately went up. I barely stopped myself from stomping out there and laying them all out before refusing them service and telling them to get out of my diner.

But it wasn't only my diner, and I was pretty sure Dani was probably holding her own and didn't need me to run in like some clumsy pseudo protector.

I composed myself, taking a moment to ask Eliot to deliver the next four cartons of eggs to Terri. And then, very calmly, I took myself out into the diner that was bustling not only with activity but tons of conversation too. I caught snatches here and there, but nothing stood out to me until I got to the table of singers.

Dani was standing there laughing, so I smoothed the glare off my face and went in with hope and an open mind.

"Not that I would have wanted her there, but she probably should have come to choir practice last night instead of skipping out. Again. Maybe then she and your mom would have kept their hands and other weapons to themselves." Andrea Farmer said and then chuckled.

"But then the chorus from 'Ding Dong the Witch is Dead' wouldn't be ringing in my head." Fanny Lewis snickered, and Dani snickered with her. That felt a little harsh, even for someone who hated her. What was going on here?

"I don't know if we have that on the jukebox, but you might try to find it." Dani patted the table twice and then turned right into me. Her eyes flashed with what I would call fire if we had been starring in a dragon fantasy novel. She hooked her arm through mine and dragged me along with her into the back room, past where Eliot was trying to organize eggs and had a stack of bread on the table. I'd have to ask him what he was doing later. For now, we had things to discuss. Like big things.

Like… "What the heck was that all about?"

"I want the choir as a whole, but definitely a few of the main members, on my list as chief suspects." She pulled an order pad out of the pocket of her apron, grabbed a pen, and started writing. "This is not going on the Spy Spindle since I don't want anyone else to see it, but there are things we need to discuss this afternoon. You heard them. They didn't actually come out and say that they think my mom did it, but they'd very much like to thank whoever finally did the deed. Who says stuff like that? A woman is dead, and they're cackling."

"Maybe it's just them being mean. If June was as awful as I keep hearing and was a part of their group, I guess they could have been in a lurch having to deal with her. We'll look into it. But it sounds like they were at practice when June was killed, so that might be an alibi for all of them."

"Fine, I'm still keeping the note, though." She lifted an eyebrow and pointed at Eliot with her pen. "Why is he dealing in eggs?" she asked.

"When I ran to the grocery store to get more eggs, I got a note on my car that was vaguely threatening. He showed up when I parked the car and saw it before I had a chance to figure out what might have happened, and so here we are."

"Wow."

"Yeah."

We stared at each other for a moment and then both started laughing at the same time.

"This isn't funny," I said between guffaws.

"You're right. It's not, but I can't stop." Dani wiped a tear from her eye and then snorted again in laughter.

"We're ridiculous." I tried to catch my breath between each word, but it just wasn't happening. So I doubled over with my hands on my knees and let the laughter roll.

Which must have concerned the people on the other side of the swinging door because all of the sudden Jeb was there in our midst and whacking me on the back.

"You okay there, girly? You got something wrong with you?"

I finally caught my breath and stood up before he could deliver another blow. "Only that my back hurts now. Why were you smacking me?"

He shrugged and smiled shyly. "I thought you might be choking or something. I'm always going to try to help you."

"Maybe not like that next time."

"What on earth was going on that you're causing such a commotion back here? I could hear you all the way up front when I walked in the door. I didn't sell this place to you after that last idiot defaulted on the loan to have it fall down around our ears because you can't handle yourself." The shy smile and shrug went to a frown pretty quickly, and I smiled at him.

"Jeb, we've been under a lot of stress. We were having a breaking moment, and instead of bawling our eyes out, we're laughing. I'm not going to apologize for that."

He harrumphed, and so I just went right over him into other things. "Did you deliver eggs the other day? I could have sworn you brought them in, and I counted them, right? But we're running out this morning, and I had to go to the grocery store to get more." I did not mention the note on my windshield since that had nothing to do with him.

He tapped his chin and shifted his gaze to the ceiling. "Actually, I was bringing them in today because I was supposed to bring them yesterday when we were going to talk about the jukebox key, but I didn't show up due to the screaming alpacas."

"Right!" Okay, phew, that made me feel so much better. Between the break-in and the new death in town, I did not want to add missing eggs on top of that noise. Me forgetting in the midst of all this chaos was far preferable to more things going wrong.

"I got them out back if you want. I tried knocking on the door. I even sent you a text despite how much I hate that kind of communication, but when you didn't answer either one, I decided to just walk around front to see what was going on. And I find you laughing like a loon."

"Fair enough. If you want to go out from here, I'll keep the door open so that you can bring the eggs in. We just had a huge order, which means we're going to need all the eggs we can get."

Eliot took it upon himself to again be the egg-cellent guy he was and followed Jeb out to the alley behind the diner to help bring in the eggs.

I left him to it and took the moment to grill Dani. "Did the choir say anything else? Anything that could be new information besides the fact that June has missed rehearsals? Is the cheeky innuendo that your mom did the killing one of the reasons you looked like you wanted to annihilate someone?"

"More than one someone. They were saying they wanted to thank whoever did it and then giving me sly looks and smiling. Fanny said it was a job they've all wanted to do for years. Of course, I told them my mom didn't do it, but they just winked and laughed, remarking that they'd heard it was a stabbing and that everyone not only knows how much she and June hated each other, but also that my mother always carries a 'sticker' in her purse in case anyone gets out of line."

I groaned. "That's not good."

"No, it's not. And my mom left me a message earlier about your dad asking her to come in for questioning today, but she refused to answer the phone. She just let him leave a message on the antiquated answering machine she refuses to get rid of. He probably tried to leave a message on her cell phone too. But she won't check those, so her voicemail is perpetually full. She won't let me clear it out either."

Hmmm, we might have to see if we could get her cell phone and password from her just to make sure there was nothing incriminating on there. I made a note on my own order pad and then shoved it back into my apron pocket.

"What did you write down?" Dani asked with a definite edge to her voice.

"A reminder to see if we can get our hands on her phone. Nothing else, I promise. We have several things going on right now, and it makes sense for us to keep track of all of it. You're still good for meeting with Eliot after work today?"

"Yes. The faster we get this handled, the faster I can go back to not wanting to strangle people for trying to throw my mother under the bus when she didn't do anything." She huffed out a breath. "At least I hope not."

Oh, I wondered when that was going to come up again. Nancy was barred from several establishments in town because she often started yelling matches and had to be escorted out. "I'm sorry this is so hard and people are being meaner than usual."

She snorted, not in laughter this time, but I continued, "Just because she has faults doesn't mean being a killer is one them." Did I really just say that? What kind of life were we living at this point if that was something that had actually come out of my mouth?

This time Dani laughed, but it was far more derisive than it had been when we were laughing hysterically.

"What if she is, though, Jax?" She pinched the bridge of her nose. "What if this really is her fault? What if she used that knife because she got angry and didn't control herself?"

I could not say the very same thought hadn't run through my own mind, so I shrugged. "That's not the way it's going to work out." I hoped. Man, did I hope, but I wasn't going to say that either.

"All we can do is search and find out who the real killer is then go from there."

"Truth."

I didn't say any more because Jeb and Eliot came back through the door carrying tons of eggs. It should be enough to tide us over for a few more days if we kept serving at this rate. Then again it was Saturday, and that was always our busiest day of the week, so we should be okay until next Saturday rolled around.

"I was going to stay and talk about the key, but you have a line out there, so I'm thinking now's not the time," Jeb said.

A line? While that, of course, made me happy, it also made me tired before I even looked at it.

"Can you come by again soon?"

Jeb nodded and then left. I was going to have to call him and arrange a time since he hadn't given a concrete answer.

So many things going on, so much to think about and process and do. I shook my head at myself and then smiled. Life was certainly not dull, at least.

Eliot chose that moment to casually pick up my hand from where it was hanging by my side and kiss my knuckles before saying, "I'll be back in a few hours with a late lunch. Don't be too tired to discuss everything."

Well then!

CHAPTER NINE

———

The rest of the work day rushed by. Closing could not come soon enough, and we actually had to chase a few people out of the diner at ten minutes past closing time because they seemed absolutely determined to linger until dinner, which we did not serve.

Eliot was due in twenty minutes, and I wanted a chance to look through what we'd accrued on the Spy Spindle before I had to share it with him. Not that I'd hide anything from him, but I wanted the option of maybe putting some of them toward the bottom, knowing we might not make it through all of them before he had to head out for work.

But he came sailing in right on time in those checkered chef's pants that had caught my eye the very first time we'd met. That time I had been afraid that, if I looked too long, I might end up seeing an optical illusion. This time I took him in from head to toe, not worrying at all that I might get caught. In fact, when I did get caught, I just gave him a smile. And he returned it with a twinkle in his eye.

"I don't have a lot of time," he said, dropping two take-out bags onto the table. "Hildy asked me to come in earlier than normal because we have a new sous chef starting, and she wants me to look him over. So let's get right down to business." He kissed me on the top of my head and then took a seat at table three as if nothing monumental had just happened.

Dani and I stared at each other and had a whole silent conversation, as besties do. We'd talk more about it later, but for the moment, my smile widened as I brought out the fruits from the Spy Spindle. The name was definitely catching on in my mind. I liked it more every time I thought of it.

I'd put the order pad slips into bundles that made sense with the various pieces of information the staff had collected today. I had several different categories. There were some rumors from the past, some info on the present things she'd been involved in at work, some info from Jess, one of the gaggle of gigglers from the theater, and a small stack of slips involving the staff at the theater. Lots to follow up on. The biggest stack, though, was for the choir. We'd start there even though I was pretty certain they all had the alibi of each other.

"So we have a bunch of people within the choir who were thanking Dani for her mom killing June. They had a practice last night that they all say they were there for. Well, everyone but June. I'm thinking we should still look into them to see if they had any other issues with her that would give them a motive to want to take her out."

Eliot crossed his arms over his broad chest and made a noncommittal noise.

"There are several leads in there to maybe chase." I shuffled a few more slips. "No matter what Dani said to them, none of them believed Nancy wouldn't have done it due to her hatred of June. Apparently, they also know about the pink knife Nancy carries in her purse."

"The alibi thing would be easy enough to check out, but you're right, we can look into each of them just in case. People will often shift the spotlight to someone else and then turn up the light in order to hide their own misdeeds in the shadows."

"Nicely said!" I did love a man who had a way with words—though I wasn't saying I loved Eliot right now since it was way too soon for that. But the way with words was a big plus in my world.

"So what do we do?" Dani asked, folding her hands on the table in front of her. She and I had chosen to sit on one side of the booth, leaving the other side open for Eliot to sprawl as he needed to for his height.

"Well, we see if there's a reason it might have been them instead. It could be a cursory probe, but it would definitely be worth it if it shines light on them and reduces the glare on your mother."

She nodded and then tapped a pen on the table. "Jax, did you see all the notes about inheritance?"

"Yeah." I grabbed that stack next. "It looks like people think June was going to come into some money from her mother's passing. Not a lot, but enough to squabble over who were the real children of her mother and who are the usurpers."

"Usurpers?" Eliot's lips moved into that half smile that made my heart trip.

"Not my word. That's what Jennifer said since they're her initials on the bottom of the paper. Maybe it was her Wordle word of the day? Regardless, she said there are five kids total, but three of them are stepchildren, and even though they've been with the family since they were little, the biological children are saying the stepchildren should get nothing. It's very nasty and was made even nastier when June waded in. Apparently, she tried to tell everyone her mother had never liked the three usurpers from the beginning and had told June privately that they would get nothing. But the will had been changed recently and in no version did she ever cut them out. She actually refers to them directly as all her children."

"Then the inheritance is possibly a good angle too." Eliot took my handful of tickets and spread them out in front of him. "The inheritance itself isn't huge, but it doesn't have to be in order for a split between five to greatly decrease what would have been a spilt between two."

"Okay, so we add the inheritance to the choir." I checked that off on my list. I grabbed the slips that dealt with the group of women who had been in the theater with us. "I'll make a note about seeing if that group of gigglers in the theater with us had anything more to add, anything they saw. I talked with them earlier and they were all going to the police station to give statements. This slip, though, says that Jess and Kimmie ran into Nancy today, and she avoided their gaze. They tried to talk with her, but she wouldn't acknowledge them."

Dani groaned. "That doesn't sound like a good thing, can we put that at the bottom?"

"She could have been concentrating on something else, Dani," Eliot said.

She simply hummed and motioned for me to continue.

"I'll put Jess, Bianca, and Kimmie on my list since I talked with them earlier." I moved a few of the slips around to find one I'd been meaning to highlight. "And we can't forget to ask about the prospects at the bank, both as fellow employees and customers. I have notes on three different people who had recently been denied loans for small businesses that, apparently, June did not want to see move here. One was a massage place, one a car repair shop, and another a hair salon."

"Oohh, lots of possibilities there! Okay, we'll keep that in mind along with the choir people and the inheritance. The suspect list just keeps getting bigger." Dani made some additional notes on her own paper and smiled.

"Anything else?" Eliot said. He'd taken the third stack of notes. "What about this ex-husband?"

That one I had hoped to ask my mom about, but maybe Dani had some info now.

"I don't remember June having an ex-husband. I don't remember a husband at all, to be honest." I turned to Dani. "You?"

She shrugged, and I wasn't sure what to make of that. I'd have to ask her later. For now, Eliot was due at his job, so he took off. Dani and I dug into the hoagies he'd brought from the deli down the street and prepped ourselves to see my mom. We'd had Marcy bring in desserts for us this week, and since I knew how much my mother loved peanut butter icing on chocolate cake, I did my duty and cut her a slice to take with us. Maybe if she was in a sugar coma, she'd answer my questions without balking too much. It was something to consider on the ten-minute drive since Dani wasn't holding up her end of the conversation, instead chewing on the sleeve of her hoodie.

"Stop that," I finally said when we pulled into my parents' driveway. My dad would be out and about at his job policing the area, so this was the best time to have my mother alone. It would be easier to pepper one Sarah Tapman with questions about the past without him there.

Once I got out of the car, I waited a few seconds for Dani to exit too. Maybe she was collecting her things and that was what was taking her longer. Whatever it was, I started walking to the front door but still hadn't heard her car door open, so I turned around and stared at her until she lifted her gaze to mine. I jerked my head toward the house, knowing that my mom had probably heard the car and would be out any moment to see what was going on.

Dani gave her head a little shake. She was not seriously telling me that she refused to get out of the car, was she? Even Stella Luna didn't do that when I took her to the vet.

I took one step toward the car to see what was holding her up, but she unhooked her seatbelt then quickly exited the passenger side.

Something was wrong, and I was not a fan of walking into my mother's house without knowing what it was or what it might turn out to be if it came out while we were here.

"What's wrong?" I reached for her hand, and she let me grab

it though it remained limp in my grasp. "You seem off, like something happened in the last twenty minutes, and I don't know what it is or why it's affecting you like this. Help me out here. I promise my dad will do everything in his power to find the right person, not just the convenient one, and he'd never send your mom to jail unless she confessed, which would be up to her. Even then, a good lawyer might be able to keep her out of the pokey due to self-defense or something." Not that I thought that was actually the case, but we could all play the tune for the time being, especially since, once it went to trial, we'd have nothing to do with the outcome.

Still not thinking like that though...

"So what's up? You do know you can tell me anything." I waited, hoping she'd open up.

"Yes, I do. Just like you knew you could tell me anything about your ex who took all your money, but you never confided in me until it was pretty much taken care of."

Oh, ouch. "That was only because I was embarrassed and thought it was all my fault. I thought I could fix it. That's not what we're dealing with here at all. There's no way I believe you did this. Besides, you never left my side from the time we got to the theater. When would you even have had time to do the deed?"

She shut her eyes and breathed out a long sigh. "I didn't do this. I promise." She looked around my parents' yard. It hadn't changed in the thirty years they'd lived here. My mom brought out new decorations for every season and holiday, so those did change but only minimally. The shrubs, the hanging baskets of fake flowers, the four rockers on the porch—all the same. It had been three rockers, but once Dani started coming over more often, a fourth just happened to conveniently show up. I'd thanked my parents that night for making her feel like a part of us, and they'd assured me she *was* a part of us, not just a feeling.

"Look, whatever is going on, you know it is a thousand times easier if we talk about it. I should have told you about the jerk ex-boyfriend and the money issues. We could have talked it out, and you wouldn't have been caught off guard. I'm sorry I didn't tell you as soon as it happened. I won't make the same mistake again."

She sighed, and I thought she could absolutely double as a bagpipe if she chose to look for a new profession.

"Fine. Before we go in then, the ex-husband is actually my mom's first husband. I really don't know what that could have to do with anything, but I didn't want your mom to tell you they'd been married and then have you think I'd been lying or something. I doubt that all these years later she and June were fighting about that, but since my mom won't tell me what they were fighting about, it might come up as a possible issue."

To say I was stunned was not powerful enough. What the heck? "Wait, so you're saying your dad is your mom's second marriage, and I've never heard this before? That's wild!"

"Why don't you girls come in here and stop having this conversation out in the front yard? Patty Mitchell just called me on the phone to let me know how long ago Nancy was married to Paul, and she just happened to be watering her plants when she heard you talk about it. It's November—no one is watering plants."

And that was my mother's final word on it as she turned back toward the house in her jeans and oversized sweater with a book tucked under her arm. We'd interrupted her reading time. I should have called ahead. Gah!

CHAPTER TEN

"To what do I owe this...pleasure?" my mom, Sarah, asked.

If there was one thing my mom did not like interrupted, it was her reading time. I knew because she said it often and loudly, usually to my dad. She wasn't mean about it at all, but she did love her reading, and if she was interrupted, she could be saucy about it. I should have checked before coming over. Not that it necessarily would have changed my timing, but at least I would have known what I was walking into and could have cut a bigger slice of cake to tide her over.

But it was too late to do that now...

She was probably just kidding with her dramatic pause, and she'd get on the information train once I told her what we were doing. Plus, if my dad had a soft spot for Dani, my mom was a jumbo-sized marshmallow of puffiness when it came to the girl that she felt she'd helped raise.

"Did you hear about June's murder?" I asked, as if she wouldn't have been one of the first to know and probably had more information than anyone else, except my dad. Although, he didn't always talk to her about cases due to the nature of his work.

"Yes, I went to the grocery store today for some milk and cookies, and I got stopped in nearly every aisle to see if I had any insider information I might want to share. I didn't—have it or want to share it, even if I did. And by the way, I'd be a little more careful about kissing in your doorway. You know I don't care, but I had to tell your Aunt Carol three times that you're old enough to not get in trouble for kissing a boy."

"Cookies?" I wheedled, trying to change the subject. I remembered at the last minute to also pop open the top on the to-go box of peanut butter icing chocolate cake.

Finally, she laughed and kissed me on the forehead then also kissed Dani on her forehead and walked toward the kitchen. Within seconds, she had us set us up with cookies and milk, and I gave her the cake.

"Why you would want those store-bought cookies when you have this cake is beyond me, but I'm grateful you handed it over so that I didn't have to tackle you for it. I could smell it as soon as I opened the front door."

I highly doubted that, but I wasn't going to fight with her when I needed intel like I did now, especially when Dani had hit me out of the blue with the ex-husband information. To say I had been unprepared for that was an understatement, and I still had to figure out where it fit in with the rest of what we knew. Could Nancy have finally snapped over everything she felt June had taken from her, down to her first husband, and it was just the final showdown? But they were no longer married, either set of people, so that shouldn't have had anything to do with the present.

Once we were all properly sugared, I held up one of my cookies and waved it in the air for emphasis as I ran my mom through the stuff with the choir and inheritance.

She listened intently, or at least I hoped so, as she closed her eyes every time she took a bite of cake and then hummed low in her throat.

"Did you hear what I just said?" I asked right after I shared that June's ex-husband had been Nancy's ex-husband first.

"Yes, I am capable of multitasking, dear, I did it for years with you, your father, and a full-time job as a nurse. I can certainly eat cake and listen to what you're saying about Nancy being a first wife and June being a second wife. And I'm sure you want to know whatever I know about the situation since we all went to high school together. I feel like I keep revisiting this same exact time period, and it's strange to have to keep going back there."

I waited until she opened her eyes again and then waited some more as she wiped the corners of her mouth, set the fork down, and then placed her hands on the table.

Then I was done waiting. "So?"

"So what?" My mother looked at me as she got up from the table and walked the container to the trash can. It took what felt like forever for her to open the lid and dispose of the container then rinse off her fork and put it in the dishwasher. It was like she was deliberately making me wait. Why?

But then Dani grabbed my elbow, sensing my irritation, and

shook her head when I looked at her. She was right. We had the time to wait her out, if that was what it took. I had interrupted her reading time after all, and if patience was the price to pay, I was going to make it rain.

She sat back down at the table after pouring herself a cup of coffee, stirring in her sugar and pumpkin spice creamer. The second that stuff hit the shelf, she'd bought vats of it for the coming months and beyond.

"I'm going to frustrate you, and I know I'm going to frustrate you, but there's nothing for it. See, we didn't run in the same circles. We weren't even friends. I wouldn't call us enemies, but we definitely never went anywhere together, and we were never on a team together. In fact, I don't even remember having any classes with June. Either her or Nancy, really. When you first brought Dani home, she looked vaguely familiar, but I wasn't sure why that would be. When I met her mom at your first playdate at their house, I knew I knew her from somewhere, but it wasn't until she started talking that it clicked. I'd know that nasally voice anywhere." She reached over and covered Dani's hand with her own. "Sorry, dear, but at least you didn't inherit that from her."

Dani smiled and gripped my mom's hand hard. "There is that."

"In other words, you're going to tell me you know nothing about anything." I was extremely disappointed. Where was the small-town vibe of everyone knowing everyone and everyone's business? I really needed that right now!

Mom stole a cookie off my plate then dipped it into my glass of milk. "I didn't say that. I wasn't going to say that either." She put the cookie in her mouth and then chewed very slowly while staring at me. She was killing me, and she knew it. But it was almost always easier to go along with her than to fight, so I flowed right along with her. Taking a cookie of my own, I also dipped and then chewed. And chewed.

"I know all about the June and Nancy show and the way they were both after the same guy in high school. That was right about when Hildy stopped talking to me and started closing herself off from the world altogether. I was shut out and had nothing else to do, so I spent all my time listening for gossip to still feel connected with what was going on. I'm not exactly proud of that time, but you didn't come by your nosiness by accident, Jax."

I almost choked on my cookie but stopped myself at the last

second. I did not want anyone else pounding on my back today. I finished the cookie, cleared my throat, and looked at her. "Do tell."

"Well, the thing is, I already told your dad. He wanted me to keep the info to myself because it might have something to do with this case he's working—the one he's willing to let you look into the gossip of while still wanting you to stay safe." She took another cookie, leaving me with only one left. "And so do I. Both of you." She looked at Dani and then back at me.

"We are going to be safe." I left out the part with the note this morning, since that person had also said they wanted me to stay safe even if it wasn't in the nicest way.

She sighed. "I know this is important to you and not just sleuthing for sleuthing's sake, but I don't think there's much in the ex-husband angle." After another dunk in my milk, she polished off the cookie. "Here's the thing. It's all just gossip. And I can't imagine that your father thinks no one else knows about it if you were to ask the right question of the right person. I guess I'm the right person this time." She smiled and then glanced over at the table where she'd placed her book.

It was a cozy mystery with an intrepid amateur sleuth who, in every book in the series, really had no business whatsoever meddling in the affairs of the cops but still managed to get the culprit every time, even if it was a little harrowing at the end.

Sound like anyone you know?

I had given it to her for her birthday a few months ago, after I'd read it first, so I knew what she was thinking about—the amateur sleuth character. The one who always found out the insider information when the cops weren't sure of who the murderer was. The one who couldn't help but admit she nailed the suspect every single time, even if she wasn't always sure she had the right person, until they started in on their monologue at the end. My mom thought I was that character and was probably casting herself as the mentor that this particular book's heroine went to in order to verify information or run theories by.

"Why are we smiling?" Dani asked. My mom hadn't taken any of her cookies, so she still had three on her plate. Since mine was empty, I stole one from her and narrowly avoided getting my hand playfully slapped before I did a quick dunk and popped the cookie into my mouth.

"Mom's about to go all in with the sharing," I replied, almost wanting to rub my hands together like a villain in an old cartoon, but then I remembered that, depending on the story, the information could possibly hurt Dani. "Are you going to be okay with whatever tea she spills?"

Dani sighed. "Here's the thing, we are all very aware of what my relationship with my family has been. I, of course, don't want it to be my mom because that would be horrendous, in general, and sad if she went to jail." She took a deep breath before continuing. "However, the thing is, and I do mean the big thing, someone has to pay for June being killed in a movie theater. Do the crime do the time, my mom used to say, so if she did the crime, then she'll have to do the time."

My mom and I shared a look because, while that might be true right now, it might not be true if we were to find out her mom was the actual killer.

"I'll tell you what," I said. "Instead of looking only for information that would prove it is someone we have in mind or, conversely, not someone we don't want it to be. Let's just prove it's the right person."

Dani stuck the cuff of her hoodie in her mouth and nodded. My mom moved it out of her mouth and then gave her a hug.

"Let's dive into the gossip. You have a notepad?" When I nodded in answer, she said, "Let's begin."

"Ready," I said, notepad and pen in hand.

"Back in the day there were two friends who were mainly in each other's pockets, not because they liked each other, but because they hated everyone else."

I started writing. It ran with Dani's mom and June as people today. Although I wouldn't have bet on them being the same now as they were then, apparently these two hadn't grown as they aged.

"So people usually avoided them as much as possible because it never failed that, if you happened to brush up against one of them, some horrible rumor, fabricated just to ruin your life, would immediately pop up. It didn't help to be nice to them either. Even the people who gave them tons of grace and space did not survive their absolute need to make sure everyone around them was miserable."

"That sounds like her," Dani said, sitting forward and writing some of her own notes. "My mom always had bad things to say regarding just about everyone. Everyone was a horrible person with a horrible life, and if I said I liked someone, for instance a teacher or the librarian, she would go out of her way to make sure I knew any and every thing they had ever done wrong. I believed her when I was very young, but as I grew up, and definitely when I came here, I was able to start seeing what she was actually doing."

I remembered those times and having to reassure Dani that a lot of those people were actually good people and that she shouldn't believe her mom.

And maybe that meant we shouldn't believe her mom now either.

Oh, boy.

CHAPTER ELEVEN

───

We left with a little more information, but that piece about not believing Dani's mom really stuck with me. Was this the right time to bring it up? I hadn't figured out a way to phrase it before Dani began talking.

"So we have at least four different directions to go here," she said.

I started up the car then saw that she had her notebook open in her lap. I considered staying in the driveway for little bit longer until I saw my Mom standing in the doorway with her book back under her arm, watching for us to leave.

"You can drive. I'm fine with reading while moving," Dani said.

"Four directions?" I asked as I put the car in reverse, and my mom waved then went back into the house. I personally couldn't read a single thing in the car or else I got motion sickness, but that was definitely one thing Dani and I very much did not have in common.

"Right, so we have the choir, which might just be a catty bunch of jerks, but we still have them even if it's just because they were mean. We have the ex-husband, which I'm super sorry I didn't tell you about earlier."

"Just a second." I pulled up to the stop sign at the end of my parents' road and turned to look at her. There was no one behind me, so it wasn't like I was holding up traffic, and this was important. "Don't beat yourself up over this. I appreciate you telling me before my mom did so that I wasn't taken off guard."

She blew out a breath. "Okay. I didn't want it to upset you."

"I promise, it didn't." She smiled, and I felt much better. Thank goodness that was over.

"Okay, so ex-husband is two, though I don't know why he would be in the running actually. I doubt he had any reason to kill his ex-wife unless she'd done something to him recently. We can still check that out. For three, we have the inheritance thing we need to get some kind of lead on. And then four, we have all these people she could have done wrong throughout the years. Maybe one of them snapped. And yes, I'm aware that one of those snappish people could have been Nancy."

Interesting that she was calling her mother by her first name. She had sometimes done the same thing when we were younger, especially when she was particularly angry at something the woman had done.

I decided not to point it out to her so that we could focus on real suspects instead of just broadly looking at the whole freaking town.

Had we somehow moved to the infamous Cabot Cove with Jessica Fletcher?

"We seem to have a bit of info on almost every lead except the inheritance," I said. "Do you want to take that for tonight, and I'll start doing some internet research on the ex and any social media about June? I'll call my dad too. I don't know if he can share anything, but it's worth trying. Plus, Eliot is already taking the business lead by agreeing to talk to Mildred."

"It's a plan, and that's better than nothing."

"It sure is. We'll keep looking." I turned onto the street behind the diner then pulled into the parking spot next to Dani's car.

"Okay, we've got this." Dani gathered her things and got out.

I waited while she stowed her belongings in the backseat then watched as she sank into the front seat of her car. When she was on her way down the road, I headed back to my own house and tried to mentally organize what to do next. Stella Luna was right where I'd left her, still nesting in the shirt Eliot had touched the other day. Silly cat…

I paced, knowing I was procrastinating calling my dad, but also knowing it had to be done.

When I sat on the couch with my phone cradled in my hands, Stella Luna came over, dragging the t-shirt with her and putting it next to me. No time like the present to call and get this over with.

My dad picked up on the third ring. "What's up, Jax?"

He didn't sound hurried or overwhelmed or even in need of getting off the phone, so I eased into the conversation.

"You home for dinner?" I asked.

"Nope, Mom sent me out for pizza and stromboli because

you gave her some book she can't seem to put down. So I'm waiting for our order and giving her a chance to finish just one more chapter."

Ha! My mother and one more chapter had been a running joke since I was little. One always turned into two, and sometimes you literally had to take the book out of her hands to make her pay attention. All good-naturedly, of course. And I could be the same way, so I wasn't faulting her.

"It gets you out of the house, though, right?" I said.

"It sure does. And doing something far more pleasant than looking into yet another murder. I just wish I could figure out what's going on around here."

I understood. You didn't grow up the kid of a cop without seeing when things bothered him.

"Have you gotten any new clues or info to help you start looking in a certain direction?"

"Not yet, and that's even more frustrating than anything else. Hang on—my number's being called."

I waited, chewing on my bottom lip and petting Stella Luna as I tried to come up with a way to tell him we had a ton of suspects but no real direction.

I heard him say a few things to Sal and knew he was just down the street right now. He could potentially bring me mozzarella sticks if I asked very nicely…

But then I heard him beep his car open and knew the chance had passed, and I'd wasted too much time as it was.

"Dad?"

"Yep, just getting in the car. Your mom asked me to grab you some mozz sticks since you're just down the way. She said you had a lot going on right now and might not remember to eat. It's a good thing you called, though, because I'm on my way to you. I'll see you in a few minutes." And he hung up.

Perfect. I could take the mozz sticks and ask my questions at the same time.

I was at the door when I saw him pull into the driveway. Sure enough, he had a small brown bag he was balancing on one hand, and he'd even brought my favorite soda with him too.

"No Stella Luna trying to dart out into the street?" Dad asked as soon as I opened the door.

I opened the door wider and gestured behind me where he could see how docile she was, cuddled up in her Eliot shirt nest.

"Nope, she has a complete and utter fondness for one of my shirts and hardly moves from it."

"Buy more of that shirt, honey." He chuckled. "Here's your dinner, though I don't think it's completely appropriate for a whole dinner. Maybe you have some salad you could eat with it?"

I scrunched my face up into a scowl, and he chuckled again. It was good to see him laugh with so much going on, especially since I was about to ask a favor.

"You have a second?" I asked.

"I…" He looked back at the running car. "Sure, of course. Let me just, um…I'll be right back."

"Dad." I caught his arm, knowing he was about to go turn off the car and, probably, text Mom that I was having some issues and that it might be good if she turned on the oven to heat their pizza back up once he got home.

There really was something so awesome about having parents who, even twenty-seven years later, thought you were important. Maybe even more important than fresh, hot pizza.

"It'll just take a second. I was going to tell you on the phone, but then you were coming here, and it's easier to just ask in person."

He blew out a breath. "Ask and we'll see if it's something I can answer. I get that you want to help, but I don't know how much I'm going to be able to share with you."

"Okay. I know you'd rather I not interfere too much, but I just have access to so many people and conversations, and I think we have four viable pools of people. I hate to dump it all on you when we could at least look into things a little bit and give you everything we find, highlighting the ones we think are more than just a possibility."

There was that chuckle I loved as he kissed my forehead. "I really had hoped that someday you'd follow me into the force. I could have sworn, with that mind of yours, that the puzzles and the justice would be something you'd love. You'd have been really good at it, but when I saw how much you loved the diner and heard you and Dani talking about owning it one day, I couldn't tell you I'd had different hopes."

I closed my eyes for just a second because I'd had no idea and didn't know what to say.

"Anyway, four 'pools' of people sounds like a lot. What does that mean?" He glanced back over his shoulder, which reminded me that his car was still running and his pizza getting cold.

"Basically, we've got inheritance issues, choir issues, job issues, and something having to do with her ex-husband."

"Any names? Any particular person in any of those pools?" He stuck his hands into his pockets and rocked back on his heels.

"No, which is the problem. Where do I start with something like that? There are twelve people in the choir. They were all at the diner this morning, telling Dani to thank her mom for offing a problem soprano. And they all have alibis because they had practice that night and everyone but June was there."

"Interesting."

"That's a very blah word said in an intriguing way." I squinted my eyes at him to see what he'd say next.

"There were actually fourteen people in the choir, and no one seems to be able to find Lori Baker since June was killed. They were rivals in the choir and had several full-out shouting matches with some pushing. So yeah. Interesting."

"Interesting, and something I think I should look into."

"Just be careful," he said. "If you get any information, I'll be grateful for it, but not if it's causing you harm."

"Understood." I let my dad go after that, knowing Sal always got their pizzas out of the oven piping hot and that, hopefully, by the time Dad made it home it would be the perfect temperature to dig right in.

Or at least that was what I told myself while I waited for my mozz sticks to cool down so I could absolutely smother them in the best marinara sauce this side of heaven.

I'd thought a time or two about being open for dinner at the Sunny Side Up. Dani and I had talked about it, but we just weren't sure if we were ready to take on all those hours and all those different foods.

As I ate, I sat with my stacks of order pad pages and got to work organizing them into my trusty notebook. I headed four different pages with the suspect groups and then the members of each group that I knew of. It didn't help much in the scheme of things since I still didn't know most of the players. For the inheritance group, I knew of two of the siblings, but not the three stepchildren, or usurpers as had been written on the paper. I texted Dani to make sure she knew who the others were and her quick response was that she had it handled because it was her job for the night. So I moved onto the next.

The choir had their very own website, which was incredibly helpful for listing out the people and doing a little bit of digging into who they were too. I was particularly interested in Lori Baker since she had not been seen since the murder per my dad. She could, of course, be out of town or just not feeling social, but she went to the top of the list. Because she hadn't posted anything on the choir's blog or her own social media in over a year, checking her out online was not helpful, but I could ask around tomorrow at the diner. Social media or not, she had more potential than the other members. Had she also been at practice with the others?

Which reminded me that I hadn't seen every person who had been in the building when June was found, and I didn't know everyone in town, beyond being able to recognize most of them by face. I decided to start a fifth page, listing everyone I remembered from that night, from the theatergoers to anyone who had stood outside while June and Nancy had played out their slap fight. Maybe I could cross-reference the names from that night with those in my other four groups. It wasn't a bad idea, but I was still working on it long after the last mozzarella stick was in my belly and my soda just watery leftover ice.

Hopefully, Dani was having better luck. I sent her a text, and she came back quickly to say she was hitting some walls but still working. Next, I texted Eliot to let him know I wasn't going to be able to come by the restaurant tonight and really didn't have anything to share anyway. He wasn't as fast to respond since he was probably in the middle of the Saturday night dinner rush, but when he did, it was just to say that he'd see me tomorrow.

An hour and four more pages of notes later, I glanced at the clock and realized it was way past my bedtime. We would be in for a big day tomorrow because it was Sunday, and the crowds would be in before church, after church, and all the times in between. But I was not complaining since we were finally growing back the steady clientele that Jeb had enjoyed when he owned the diner. It was just a lot of work.

I went through my nightly routine, leaving Stella Luna with her shirt nest, and headed for bed with thoughts of murder in my head. Real murder took some serious grit, and I couldn't think of anyone on any of my lists who'd rather risk life in prison than let June walk around one more day.

I laid down and stared at the ceiling for a little while, making a mental note that I should probably consider doing a deep clean of my place soon.

Then again, the diner was making a lot of money lately, and maybe I could see about just paying someone else to do the job.

I drifted off thinking about walking into a pristine house that I could just enjoy instead of busting my rear end over but was startled awake by the sound of yowling.

Jumping out of bed, I darted into the living room and then sank onto the couch when I saw Stella Luna. She was in a fury because the shirt had gotten stuck on the edge of the door when she'd tried dragging it around a corner.

My heart was thundering in my chest, and I wasn't certain if I'd ever be able to breathe evenly again, but at least it was nothing.

"Holy cow, girl. You are going to give me a heart attack! It's a shirt. You could have just curled up there." But I knew my dear Stella was totally against that. She wanted things the way she wanted things, and there was absolutely no compromise. Ever.

I trundled off the couch, stumbling around a few toys she had scattered on the rug then almost slipping on an order pad paper. It looked like she had knocked all of those off the table too. This cat. She was lucky I loved her!

I shuffled through the slips of paper in an effort to reorganize before giving up because it was the middle of the freaking night, and I had to get up in an hour to go to work. Gah!

I laid back down and with thoughts of Eliot swirling in my poor brain, I drifted off to sleep only to be yanked right back out by my alarm.

I groaned. Couldn't I just go back to bed? Forget that I existed anywhere but in my little cave?

Fat chance of that.

So I prepared myself for the day. Once I was ready, I kissed Stella on her head and got another whiff of Eliot from the t-shirt. Whatever cologne he wore had staying power even though it wasn't overwhelming in any way.

Yum.

I left before I could sit on the floor and lay my head down next to her so that we could both just chill.

When I arrived at the diner, no one was in the back parking lot. Terri was probably on her way, and I'd have to look at the schedule to see who else was supposed to be here this morning for the first shift.

At least we had eggs and, as far as I knew, everything else we needed to make today another one for the books. I looked forward to hearing lots of gossip.

After unlocking the door, I ran for the keypad, hoping, as I did every day, that I'd manage to get the code put in before alarms started blaring and the cops came out to see what kind of mischief I'd managed this time.

The whole thing went off without a hitch, fortunately, but it did make me pause and think about who had been trying to break in the other day. Why here, and for what? It wasn't like we had a huge till, and while we might have a bunch of food in here, it wasn't stuff you couldn't get right down at the grocery store or at one of the local farms. We weren't Hildy with her lobsters and high-grade steaks. We did have high-quality syrup, but I very much doubted anyone really knew that or would risk getting caught and going to jail for it.

But people did weird things for weird reasons. With the intruder only being in the diner for less than thirty seconds before the alarm went off, there wouldn't have been much of a chance for the person to take anything.

I kicked on the grill and flipped on the lights, started the coffee, made sure the wrapped silverware bin was full, and that the menus were stowed correctly. The crew began streaming in five minutes later. There was a lot of chatter, and it sounded very much like something had happened that I'd missed. I waited for them to all get to their stations before I cornered Terri.

"What's everyone talking about, and why are you all so animated at this god-awful hour?" The sun still hadn't come up yet, and I hadn't even had my first cup of coffee. No one should be talking as much as they all were.

"They arrested someone for June's murder last night. The person walked right into the station and admitted to killing her, but no one seems to know why. I'm surprised you didn't hear about it."

"What? They arrested someone? Who is it?"

"Jennifer posted it in the chat we have, and then everyone started chiming in about how weird it was."

"Why was it weird? Wait, you have a chat?"

She rolled her eyes and moved me out of the way. "Don't get sidetracked, Jax. They arrested someone for June's murder, so we don't have to use the spindle anymore. Everything can go back to normal. Well, at least our normal, which is not normal, but that's beside the point."

"Did Jennifer put that we're not normal in the chat too?" I leaned against the counter, fully aware I was not helping.

"Off track. Don't you want to know who they arrested and why they arrested her?"

The use of the word "her" did not sound like a good thing and neither did Terri's need to tell me right now. I would freely admit, even if only in my head, that I actually felt sick about knowing who they had arrested because I was afraid I would not be okay with the answer.

Terri stared at me. She wasn't just going to say it. She was going to make me ask.

"Who?"

"Mildred Case."

Well, that was not the woman I was dreading, at least not this time. Huh.

CHAPTER TWELVE

I wandered away from Terri once she'd divulged the name of the supposed killer. Mildred Case. Mildred Case? She went into a movie theater and knifed a woman in her seat? I just was not getting my brain to wrap around that.

She had been at the theater, though, and Eliot said she had talked to him that night.

But Mildred? She was not exactly a spring chicken, and she'd been heading into the theater for the newest drama at a different run time, according to the information Eliot had shared. I'd heard the movie was meant to make you bawl your eyes out. When would she have had time to sneak into our movie without being seen and then stick a knife in June before quietly returning to her seat in the tearjerker?

I didn't think I could believe it. I doubted my dad would have taken her seriously, except that she'd turned herself in. No way would he believe she really had done the deed. Her name hadn't come up at all in any of the Spy Spindle notes yesterday. So weird!

But he'd have to take her in even without evidence to back it up if she'd given a valid confession. I wanted to know what she'd said even though I couldn't exactly demand he tell me everything.

And yet, I could call and tell him I had information on a suspect while playing dumb on the Mildred angle and see what he said…

I didn't get a chance to do that, though, for the next couple of hours. We got slammed with customers, of course. It was Sunday morning and our regulars who came in before church or in between services were joined by many in the community who now believed we were the hub of all good gossip. I jumped in as head bus girl, something I knew I had always done well, unlike filling sugar containers and making toast. My dish removal and cleaning rag swipe at a table were unmatched and always had been.

After I cleaned table twelve, I went back to table ten and then on to table four. With each swipe and clean, I felt better, especially as our hostess for the day seated people at pristine tables with well-wrapped silverware, wonderfully polished tabletop jukeboxes, and correctly filled sugar and salt containers. I'd had someone else fill those and had absolutely no guilt over that.

Being on bus-girl duty was an excellent way to pick up all the latest bits of gossip and hearsay without being noticed. Soon enough, I had to start stealthily jotting down notes on my order pad to keep from forgetting the finer details, like who had said they'd seen a red car racing down the street after the movies.

I also heard more about some guy who had wanted to start up a car repair shop, which I initially ignored, until I remembered that there was a loan June had denied that involved a repair shop not meeting her standards. After I'd heard mention of him for the fifth time, I had to get the lowdown.

"Who is this Jonathan Stilton?" I asked Bert, a local who usually knew all the players in town, as I topped off his coffee for the fourth time. I probably should have cut him off, but if he wanted to be so caffeinated he was buzzing in his seat, it wasn't my place to tell him no.

"You've never heard of Jonathan Stilton?" Bert stirred six packets of sugar and five creamers into his mug. After all the years I'd served him, I knew his routine and had only given him half a cup of the dark liquid to allow the room to make it into a blonde bombshell.

"I haven't," I said, leaning against the counter. "I wouldn't have asked if I had."

"Touché." He smiled, and I settled in. That smile almost always meant there would be a story with rabbit holes, squirrel runs, and the conversational equivalent of a chat with a toddler who had an obsession he must absolutely share with you. However, if he had info I might need, I was here for it.

"I'm surprised you haven't heard anything about this guy since he was one of the first people your dad had a hand in taking off the streets."

"Are you talking thirty years ago because, in case you don't remember, I'm not quite in that decade yet."

"Another touché. I might need to get myself some protective gear with the slashes you're making."

I laughed, because I was supposed to, and then waited for him to finally dive into what he actually wanted to share.

"He used to run a repair shop with his dad, but they went bankrupt when the bank wouldn't let them extend their loan. His dad ended up dying shortly after from a heart attack, and Jonathan went on a rampage, burning the place down to the ground and telling the bank it could take the insurance money and shove it. I don't know why he got so many years when, if I remember correctly, there were no human casualties. It was just pricey. He's been out of jail for about six months now and was trying to get another shop up and running, but no one will give him a loan, and any money his dad left him is long gone."

"And June was the one who denied the loan?" I asked. Dani raised her hand at the front counter, and I knew I'd have to leave in a few seconds, but I wanted to let Bert finish this out.

"That's what I heard. He tried to go to the other bank in town, but he's a liability, and no one was playing his game. June had led him on at one point, though, telling him she'd make it work since long ago they'd had an affair, but in the end, she was just stringing him along. Rumor has it she denied him and wrote the word *Karma* across the application.

"Wow, that's harsh. Did anyone hear him threaten her after the denial? Could that be a motive for him to serve up his own kind of karma?"

"Are you looking into that?"

I glanced away and then back. "No, not really."

But I seemed to have not said the words forcefully enough because he laughed and then motioned for me to refill his mug.

Dani waved again. I did not have any more time to dillydally. She was going to come over and see what I was up to if I didn't get moving.

I nodded at Bert and thanked him then hustled over to Dani.

"What can I do for you?" I asked as I stood on the opposite side of the counter from her.

"I need to know if you're hearing anything important." She blew out a breath. "My mom has texted me seven times in the last thirty minutes, and I need to be able to say if we're finding anything to clear her name. She said that even though they've arrested Mildred, she is still getting snubbed and harassed."

I shrugged and dipped my hand into my apron pocket, bringing out my stash of info from today. "I've got some notes but nothing concrete, although we might have something to look into from the banking perspective. Can't you just tell her we're doing everything we can and leave it there?"

"I tried that." She smiled at Melanie Jessup and her cronies as they came in and took up seats at the counter near Bert.

"What happened when you tried? Wasn't it enough?" But I kind of knew what her answer was going to be before she even said it.

"She wants real information, and she wants your dad to come to the house and tell her specifically that he will stop looking at her. She thinks I should take every day off work until I dig far enough in to make sure her name is totally removed from the suspect list."

I blew out a breath. "We're not going to be able to do that, and I can't make my dad stop looking just because that's what she wants. Plus, if Mildred actually did it, then it's over anyway."

"I don't believe that, and neither do you. Besides, you know Nancy is going to want her name cleared, along with a formal apology. I feel terrible for your dad until this gets solved because she's on a tear, and that can't be fun for your dad."

"Meh, he can handle it. Let's try to find something to tell her to get her off your back. I'm going to keep clearing tables, and I'll keep an ear out. Promise."

When I started to walk away, I heard Dani gasp and turned back in time to see her run around the counter to hug Ian. She ushered him and three of his friends to table three and then handed out menus, hanging around for just a few extra seconds to run a hand from Ian's shoulder to his fingertips.

I was so happy to see her happy, especially in the midst of all this drama.

Focusing back on the tables, I got to cleaning and listening in. I even heard some more about this Jonathan guy. It appeared that most of the women were very pleased that he had aged well in jail. According to them, he was as debonair when he got out as he had been going in. They labeled him a bad boy, and I had to keep walking so that I didn't comment on how horrible the bad boy really could be.

At that point, I started just taking the pad out and writing right where I was. No one was paying attention anyway, and that was fine with me.

Fortunately, Eliot chose that moment to stroll in through the front door and seated himself at the counter. Maybe he could help me get out of this spiral.

"Milkshake coming up," I said as I buzzed behind him. "And I'm going to need you to drink it in the other room if you don't mind."

He followed me with his gaze, watching me walk by him, around the end of the counter, and then back to him.

"But I was hoping to play a song on the jukebox."

I rolled my eyes. "I'll plug one in for you if you'll follow me to the side room."

"Fine."

Saucy. But he grinned at me, so all was forgiven. I caught Dani in the pass-through to the back and gripped her hand. "Eliot is here. If you don't mind watching over everything, I'd like to go in the side room."

"Will the door be closed? Do I need to randomly check on the two of you to make sure there's nothing untoward going on? Because I will. I promise I will." She raised an eyebrow at me, and I smirked at her.

"Did you hear about Mildred?" the guy behind me said.

"Yeah, there's no way she'd have done something like that, though. She's old and doesn't have the physical capacity to actually hurt anyone, much less stab them. I mean, come on. I had to take her groceries out of her car the other day because she was having some muscle trouble and couldn't pick up the few bags she had." He scoffed. "I'll tell you what, the cops around here don't seem to know what they're doing anymore, and that makes me mighty concerned." The last part he said almost as a whisper, but my bat ears picked up on it, and I wasn't going to let it pass.

Shutting off the shake machine, I left the shake glass on the counter, knowing myself and the fact that I didn't want to accidentally chuck it at Wallace Youngston's head if he said anything else I wouldn't be able to let pass.

"Mr. Youngston, surely you are not suggesting my father would arrest someone without cause? You can't really think my father would decide to take a woman, or anyone, into custody without facts to back it up."

The front door opened, and the man of the hour walked in as if he was on a serious mission. Reading the room, he immediately came to the counter where he stopped, resting a hand on Wallace's shoulder.

"How's it going here today?" my dad asked, looking between Wallace and his friend Edgar.

Both had the grace to blush a little and dart their gazes away.

"Dad, I've had a couple of questions today about Mildred turning herself in. Did you find something, or did something happen that made you believe it really could be her?"

For his part, my father slow blinked. I'm sure he would have rather closed his eyes completely and sighed or, conversely, smacked the heads of the two men in front of him together.

"I'm glad you asked, sweetie."

I almost pointed to my name tag as he had at the theater when he wanted me to call him by his professional name. But this was too serious to make jokes. I'd say something later if I remembered.

"So what's going on then?" Edgar asked.

"Mildred is not under arrest nor will she be. She came in stating she had been the one to kill June, but she didn't know any of the details. She didn't even know which movie June had been watching. I'm not entirely certain what the purpose of turning herself in was, but we'll be assigning her someone to get her some aid."

Now Wallace's ears flamed red, and he quickly excused himself to the restroom. He stopped at three different tables, probably to share that Mildred had not in fact been arrested, before disappearing into the door marked *Restroom*. Good enough.

"You have any other questions, Edgar?" Dad asked as he took Wallace's seat, pushing the plate of creamed chipped beef on white toast out of his way.

"No, sir," Edgar said.

"Good." My dad rested his elbows on the counter then peeked behind me. "Any chance you could put that shake into a to-go cup for me and make another one, Jax?"

"Sure. Eliot won't mind."

"Eliot's here? Make a second one then and come along. Is he in the side room?"

I nodded then did what I was asked as he walked away. Once I had both shakes ready, Wallace returned to his seat and pulled his plate back in front of him. So how would he handle this?

"Sorry, Jax. I hope you didn't say anything to your dad about me."

Edgar shook his head and put his napkin on the counter.

"You're a dolt, Wallace. Of course, she didn't say anything. Jax knows what happens at the counter stays at the counter, and you deserve for her to rat you out to her dad, but she's better than that. No one needs your gossiping."

Oh, now hold on. I wanted all of their gossiping. "You know what, Edgar, I appreciate that, but honestly, people talking about things in the diner gives me a chance to know what's going on in town. Plus, if I know something to prove or disprove a rumor, then I like being able to help our community."

Edgar winked at me with his right eye, which was not on the side Wallace was sitting on.

I left them to the rest of their breakfast as I walked to the side room. Lifting one of the shake cups to Dani, I saluted her as I walked past.

"I'm not going to worry about what you're doing since I just watched your dad walk in," she said and then had the audacity to laugh.

I wanted to roll my eyes at her, but I was afraid I might hurt myself. Instead, I braced myself for whatever I was about to walk into.

I used my rear end to bump the door open and then turned to find them both reading over the songs different jukeboxes had to offer and laughing together. They stopped as soon as they realized I was there, both straightening up and clearing their throats at the exact same time. I knew there was a thing about marrying someone like your dad, and mine was a wonderful example of what I should have been looking for in a relationship all along, but this was a little too close for comfort. At least they were dressed differently—Eliot in his jeans and a t-shirt with some band on the front and my dad in full uniform. But the alikeness beyond that was a little daunting.

"Here you go. Now let's get down to business. Who knows what?" I said, taking the lead and daring anyone to try to pry it out of my cold hands. I couldn't say cold, dead hands since they weren't dead, just nearly frozen from transferring the shakes.

I crossed my arms and tucked my hands into my armpits, waiting to see what happened next.

CHAPTER THIRTEEN

"Before we get into that, I wanted to tell you that we found your burglar about an hour ago," my dad said as he took a seat in the side room we primarily used as storage.

"Seriously? That's wonderful. Who is it?" If it was someone I knew, I was definitely going to have to deal with feeling incredibly insulted.

"One of our internet guys got a tip that there was a video online of a kid boasting that he took a dare and ran with it. Jeff down at the station recognized the back of the building in the video, and since the kid wasn't smart enough to not post his name, we were able to trace it to a high schooler in town. I've talked with his mom, and they're coming in later today to discuss damages and the punishment. We're thinking community service."

"Part of me is happy it wasn't more serious, but what is it with these internet challenge things? It's so destructive for nothing but some likes."

"It's an issue, but I'm glad it wasn't something worse, either."

"True. Community service might be just the thing for a punishment, but I think you should also add a fine to make the lesson stick. He could post that on whatever social media he has. Maybe it will warn other people to be smarter."

"One can hope," Dad said.

Back to the other topic at hand then. "Did you know the guys were talking about you when you first came in?" I asked. "Or were you just guessing when you came in and arrowed right in on Wallace?"

He sighed. "Yes, I'd heard some talk around the station that Wallace was trying to cause issues with the investigation, wanting to know why we hadn't caught anyone yet. Apparently, he and June had circled each other for years over a variety of things. They're neighbors—and enemies because of it."

"Why am I not surprised?" I wrote that down too. I was going to run out of order pads at this rate. I had my notebook at home, but I wasn't comfortable using it while I was working and had nowhere to conveniently stash it like the order pads.

"I've never had this many suspects in my whole career, to be honest, and each of them has the means and the motive, depending on how angry they were and how recent the wrong was. I did hear that the ex is out of town, so at least that's one less person to keep an eye on." Dad took another slurp and then shifted in his seat at the table where the unused jukeboxes still sat.

I really needed to get in here and clean things up, but it felt very low on my to-do list at the moment.

"So at this point, you have a bunch of people who might have done it but no real way of knowing who might be the actual killer?" I asked.

"Precisely," my dad said then finished off his shake. "Speaking of that, I need to get back to it. Let me know if your gossipers out there come up with anything that might help me narrow things down."

"Of course," I said and then hugged him before he walked back out to the diner proper. Which then left me alone with Eliot. I smiled at him, and he drank more of his shake.

"I know that smile," he said. "You have an idea?"

"Several actually, but first…" And I stepped into his personal space and laid a kiss on him he wouldn't soon forget. Dani and her open-door threat could just stay out in the diner where they belonged.

"Better than the shake," Eliot said as we broke apart after a minute.

"Glad to hear it." I chuckled.

His laugh was low. "On to investigation things. I'm still trying to get in touch with Mildred. She avoided my calls the first few times I attempted to reach her, and now that she's turned herself in for the crime even though she didn't do it, she might not want to talk at all."

"If anyone can reach her, it's probably you."

"You might think that, but I don't believe she does anymore. I'll try anyway. Nothing to lose, especially if you think she might like me."

I thought about telling him that even Stella Luna adored him and was currently nesting in the shirt I'd worn that smelled like him, but his phone rang.

He flipped the device over on the table. "Gotta take this. I'll be back after you close." And then he gave me a quick kiss and headed out the door with his phone to his ear.

I took a moment, or maybe two, to sigh in pleasure. It was as nice watching him walk away as it was watching him walk toward me, especially when I knew I'd see him again in about an hour. I could get used to that…

Dani swung around the door frame to smile at me. "I didn't even check on you once I saw your dad leave and close the door again behind him. I want points for that."

I laughed and then shrugged my shoulders. "You can have all the points."

"Excellent! I also need all the help I can get out here. We're knee deep in people, and we close in an hour. We need to get them fed and cashed out so that we can meet with Eliot, and then I have plans tonight to hang out with Ian."

"When did that happen?"

"He asked me after he and his friends were here for breakfast." The adorable blush on her cheeks made me so happy for her.

"That, too, is excellent." I stuck my hands in my apron pocket and pulled out the many slips I had. Part of me wanted to spear them on the Spy Spindle if only to show that I was working as hard as I thought everyone else should be working. But I also wanted a chance to go through them myself before I stuck them on the spike.

"Did you find anything out from your dad about Mildred? That seems like the only thing most people are talking about today."

"Just that they were sending her off with help because she didn't know anything other than gossip about the killing. Eliot is going to try to talk with her, but he doesn't think she wants to talk with him anymore. And Dad found the guy who tried to break in at the diner on Friday. Some internet challenge thing on social media. He's a teenager, so they're thinking a fine and community service." I stuck the slips back in my pocket. I'd deal with them after we closed.

"Oh, that makes me feel so much better."

"Yeah, me too. Hopefully we won't have to worry about something like that again."

"And good luck to Eliot. He's probably going to need it. Now can you please get out here so that we can close down on time?

My stepdad just walked in, so I'm going to say hi, and then I'll get back to work too."

She held the door open as I scooted past her and walked out to find Kimmie and her cousin Jess taking the dishes from two tables and stacking them in the dish tub right outside the swinging doors to the back.

What were they doing? I rushed to their side and reached out for the dishes. No one should be bussing their own tables. Ever. I didn't want anyone to think we weren't capable of managing our own diner. Yikes!

"Hey, I've got this," Kimmie said with a smile and proceeded to stack the dishes in the tub exactly how I liked.

"You don't have to do that. I'm so sorry your table wasn't taken care of earlier."

"No problem. Really, we're happy to help. Aren't we, Jess?"

"Absolutely! I used to work here when the last owner was doing those smoothie things. The menu was horrible, but I really liked the job." She took a hairband off her wrist and used it to pull back her blonde hair into a ponytail. Were they settling in to be bus girls?

I looked over to Dani, who shrugged and then went to answer Terri calling her into the kitchen.

"Well, it's appreciated but not necessary." I should have been out here doing my job instead of talking with my dad and Eliot and then sighing over Eliot. Dang it!

Jess offloaded her last set of perfectly stacked cups and then leaned on the counter next to me. "In all seriousness, Jax, I want to thank you for all I've heard you're doing to hopefully bring June's killer to justice. I was sad to see her go even though she wasn't always the nicest person. We had been working on some things together, so I guess we're back to square one. Now we'll have to deal with Mildred, though of course that's not as horrible as being dead."

"I'm sure things will work out for you, Jess," Kimmie said and hugged her cousin. "But we really do appreciate all you're doing, Jax. I just hope you're staying safe. I heard about a note on your car. That must have been scary."

"I'm not really looking into anything in particular," I lied. "We're just filling in whatever info we can." I didn't mean to glance over at the nearly full Spy Spindle, but I didn't stop myself in time.

"Yeah, I asked our server, Jennifer, what that was earlier,"

Jess said. "What a great idea to keep track of all the gossip. Like those podcasts I listen to all the time, maybe someone will slip up and say something that will break the case wide open!"

"We can always hope," I said, smiling at her enthusiasm.

"Jess, we should go." Kimmie hooked her arm through Jess's bent elbow. "If you need any help at all, Jax, just let us know. I have free hours in the morning now that I'm down to part-time at work, until things get moving again with my cousins. And as much as I'm aware that June wasn't the easiest of people to deal with, she didn't deserve to die that way. After we gave our statements to the police, they told me they were looking at all suspects. But I got the impression they didn't really have anything concrete, so I'm grateful you're also helping. Somehow it feels like we owe June that since we were there when she was killed. Does that make sense?" She pushed a button on the jukebox on the counter next to her, looking down as if she was afraid she'd sound stupid and didn't want me to see her face.

I patted the back of her hand. "Actually, yes, it does, and I understand. It makes it feel less like you're totally out of control."

She nodded as she continued pushing buttons. "I'm serious on that offer to help out around here. I'm sure I could help fill that info thing. I'm a good listener and people sometimes don't notice I'm around. I'm like a ninja," she said with a big goofy smile when she finally looked up at me.

I laughed but didn't tell her it was called the Spy Spindle since that sounded like we were spying on our diners. Which, of course, we were, but I didn't really want them knowing about it.

"I'll talk to Dani and let you know. We appreciate the offer."

"Sure thing," Kimmie said, and they stopped by to pick up Bianca, Jess's sister, at their table then left, thankfully, without bussing another table.

The next hour passed with the Spy Spindle not getting much new info. It seemed Birdie Candra had managed to not only run a stop sign but also race away from the cops in her 1993 Pontiac Sunbird before almost crashing into a fire hydrant and coming to rest against a tree. She'd only bumped it, so it wasn't like she demolished her car, but the diner was all atwitter about what she had been doing, not to mention why she chose to run in the first place.

Finally, we were able to close the diner and count the receipts. Dani's stepdad was one of the last people to leave, and he kissed her on the cheek as he said goodbye. As always, his voice was incredibly quiet and his words were tinged with a sadness that Dani had told me came from having to deal with her mom all the time. I had my thoughts on why he didn't just leave, but I didn't know for sure, and that was a mystery we weren't going to solve today.

It was good to see that not only were more people coming in, but they were coming in consistently. And it wasn't only murder talk that got them in the door, as today proved.

Dani and I high-fived once we were able to sort out what our bank deposit was going to be then set about making ourselves grilled cheeses before Eliot was due in.

"It was a good day," she said as she got out plates and stood ready with the knife.

"It absolutely was. And we've got some good info to go over. Did you get anything in particular?" I used my spatula to peek at the corner of the grilled cheeses on the grill. Not quite as golden as I liked, but it was getting there.

"Not really, but at least my mom stopped texting after I told her we have new leads we're looking into. I didn't know if what I was saying was true, but I did it anyway. And I'm not ashamed to admit it."

"Ha! Serves her right."

Dani looked to the front of the diner and giggled. "You have a visitor. He looks like he might be drooling out there. Either over your masterpiece grilled cheeses or perhaps it's you…"

She walked away to get the door while I finished up what I was doing and relished the idea of Eliot perhaps drooling over me. I wouldn't say no, let's just leave it there.

Once she opened the door, they stood talking for a minute while I finished up the sandwiches. I had no idea what they were talking about, but they glanced at me a few times and were both laughing and snickering like children.

If I gave Dani the slightly more than golden brown grilled cheese, that had happened only because she'd distracted me, then it was her own fault.

"Milkshake?" I asked as I plated the sandwiches.

"Not for me," Dani said.

Eliot smiled. "Nope, I'm still full from the last one."

We took the booth right near the front door. Dani and I sat on one side across from Eliot to give him the space he needed as always. We all dug into our sandwiches, and I was probably a little too pleased at the murmurs of delight over what amounted to two pieces of bread, some butter, and good cheese. But after everything that had been happening recently, it was enough to make my whole day.

"I think we got some good info today even with having to listen endlessly to the newest scandal going around about Birdie making a run for it from the police and then hitting a tree." I gave both of them the rundown about what I'd heard about Jonathan then turned to Dani. "I didn't get much from my internet searching last night, did you? Is there any real threat in the inheritance angle?"

"Nope, it's nothing. The will had never been changed. In fact, the whole estate was liquidated six months ago. I ended up being friends on social media with pretty much everyone involved, and when I sent them messages, they all came back saying they'd heard the same thing and that none of it was true." She shook her head and took another bite of the triangle of bread and cheese. There really was no other way to cut the sandwich but diagonally, and don't let anyone tell you any different.

"Eliot?"

He put his sandwich down and wiped his fingers on his napkin. "Actually, I did get a chance to talk to your dad for a bit after we left. I knew you were wondering what exactly happened with Mildred, so I cleared it up with him. She turned herself in because she's afraid she's running out of money from some relative who keeps asking for help. She thought if she got put in jail that at least she'd be taken care of and wouldn't be in a position where she'd have to say no to them but also not have to keep saying yes."

What on earth? I tapped the back of the vinyl booth and watched Dani sort through the papers on the spindle. "Seriously?"

"Yep. Your dad said it took some time, but he got everything worked out. He told her that, if they bother her again, she can call him, and he'll take care of it. I'm still trying to follow up with her myself to talk about her information regarding June's financial decisions making people mad, but I thought I'd give her a few hours." And then he took the last bite of his sandwich. I watched his jaw work and then his throat. Unfortunately, I watched long enough for Dani to feel the need to poke me under the table.

I was about to retaliate, but Dani derailed my train of thought when she squeaked in her seat next to me.

"Who is using an orange crayon to write out things for the Spy Spindle?" she asked, holding up an order slip that didn't look like any of the others. Orange words were scrawled on the paper, the handwriting jagged and huge.

"No one," I said quietly as I took the paper out of Dani's hand and rubbed my pointer finger over the waxy words.

"What does it say?" Eliot craned his head to see the writing.

"Table Three Songs Help," I read aloud then turned it over, looking for any additional clues or writing. "At least it's not a threat this time."

"Well, you hope it's not a threat, but what does it mean?" Dani plucked the note out of my hand, and I scooted out of the booth to visit table number three.

I flipped the cards in the jukebox on the table back and forth, looking for something out of the ordinary but finding nothing. None of the song titles seemed to be phrases that would point in a new direction. I pressed all the buttons next, wondering if something would pop out. Dani slid onto the bench across from me and checked the top then ran her fingers along the back where it was attached to the wall.

"Anything?" I asked.

"Nothing." She smacked the top of the machine with the side of her fist and something clinked and then slid out onto the table from beneath the jukebox.

A small white envelope with my name on it in orange waxy crayon.

To quote my dad: Interesting.

CHAPTER FOURTEEN

———

I was quicker than Dani, so I grabbed up the small envelope before she even blinked.

"Dang, girl," Dani said, then laughed. "Quickest one gets it all."

"But what is it?" Eliot asked, leaning a hip against the booth opposite me.

I turned the white envelope over and over to see if there were any significant markings on the outside but found nothing. There was something inside the envelope, though—something more than just paper.

"Hopefully not a threat." Nervously, with my eyes almost shut as if that would protect me, I slid my finger under the edge of the flap. Considering the possibility of a paper cut, I wiggled my finger slowly along the edge but then got impatient with myself and ripped the rest open. My desire to know what was in it was far more important than worry about a papercut.

As I removed the piece of folded paper from the envelope, a key dropped out and pinged on the table before skidding toward Dani. She grabbed it up and inspected it while I read the words, again written in orange waxy crayon.

"You're not on the right trail yet, but maybe this will help."

"What on earth?" Dani plucked the note out of my hand.

"I have no idea what it means. Do you think it's the same person who called about the key I found last week in the other jukebox? Should I call Jeb?"

"No, let's hang on a minute," Dani said. "The envelope has your name on it, and the note was put on the Spy Sindle today, so why would it have anything to do with Jeb? I think it's about this current murder."

"Okay, I can see that." I leaned forward with my elbows on the table then looked up at Eliot. "Thoughts?"

"It has to have been put there today. You collect the tickets from your spindle every day, right?"

"Yes."

"And the paper was put on the spindle today?"

"Also, yes," Dani said.

"Then do we know who sat at table three today?" Eliot asked.

Dang it, why hadn't I installed those freaking cameras like I told my dad I would?

I put my head on the table and sighed.

"Well, hang on another minute." Dani poked me in the shoulder, and I simply rolled my forehead to the side to look at her without actually lifting my head. I'd wipe the table down later.

"What am I hanging on for? I don't know what this means or who is leaving these clues."

"First of all, I do not like your attitude, so you're going to need to change that immediately." She poked me in the arm again and smiled at me.

Eliot had the audacity to chuckle at that. I raised my head and gave him the stink eye at that point, but he only let his smile grow wider and tilted his head over to Dani. Traitor.

"Second, we have been putting the table numbers on the tickets for some time now, so if they used a credit card, we'll possibly be able to find out who sat here and might have left the note and key. Table three was busy today. I seated Ian and his friends here, and then my dad took the table when you were talking with your dad and Eliot in the side room. In between, the table was always occupied by a number of other people. We can sort out who else would have sat here and had access to leave this note."

She was not wrong, which made my spirits lift a little.

"Third, even if we don't find out exactly who was here, at the very least, this is not a threat. And someone thinks you are capable of getting on the right track, which is different than the last time we were looking into things."

Also not wrong, but I was not willing to tell her she was right just yet.

"Fourth, and finally." She nudged my shoulder again with her finger. "We have resources galore. Let's see where this leads us."

"You're such a ray of sunshine," I said with straight-out dry wit, and this time she didn't just use her finger but her whole hand to lightly swat me on the shoulder. I couldn't stop myself from grudgingly giving a little laugh as I sat back in my seat.

Turning the key over in my hand, I found a three-digit number on the back along with a name. *Portman*. Where had I heard that before? Was it the last name of the person who owned the key? The name of the building where I'd find whatever this key went to?

"Here, you look it over," I said, handing the key to Eliot. "I'm going to make myself a milkshake. Perhaps that will bring about the attitude change Dani thinks I so severely need."

She giggled, which was enough to send me right out of the booth and over to the machine on the other side of the counter.

That key could be the…well, the key to everything. But where did I start looking? More importantly, why couldn't the person have been more explicit with what they meant if they really were trying to help me?

I sent the blender into overdrive but realized a second too late that I did not have the metal cup in hand as well as I thought I had. Ice cream, syrup, and milk flew out of the cup and landed on my face, chest, and hands. It also left me sputtering and laughing loudly, for real this time.

"Someone come help me help myself," I sputtered.

They were already on their way, also laughing at the mess I had yet again caused. It always seemed to be something with me.

"I might want to rethink this whole owning a diner thing when I not only can't tell the difference between sugar and salt and can't make toast properly, but now I've also managed to mess up the one thing I've prided myself on for years. I should not be allowed to touch anything." I could have been crying at all my missteps, but instead I chose to belly laugh as Dani got a rag to wipe down my front. Eliot took the metal cup out of my hand and used another rag to wipe down the counter in front of me, the counter behind me, and then finally the floor where I'd managed to whip out tons of chocolate-looking sludge.

"You're doing fine, Jax, and you know it," Dani said. "This only seems to happen when you're distracted, so maybe it's just a reminder to keep your thoughts under control and not let things sit so hard on you that you aren't paying attention to what's right in front of you?"

I was so thankful Dani had said that because she was right. I'd take it and use it to get myself back on track.

"Portman," I said abruptly as a chime rang in my brain. "Isn't there a Portman Storage over on Grosse Street? Aren't they relatively new?" Our town center had stayed small and old, but more and more the town itself was expanding out into what used to be farmland and was now copious storage facilities and car washes.

"Yesssssss!" Dani said, dropping the rag to pull out her phone. I was abandoned and only half clean, but I did not want Eliot wiping my t-shirt with a towel, so I picked up what Dani had thrown down and finished the job myself. Fortunately, I had extra clothes in the back room in my locker. I quickly made my excuses, which probably no one heard, and left for the back. Dani and Eliot were completely engrossed in looking at Dani's phone and comparing notes on where this clue could lead, and why someone would have left the key here.

I admittedly felt like this whole thing was along the lines of a new wild goose chase. I did not like geese and chasing was at the very bottom of my list of favorite things to do.

But this appeared to be what we were stuck with. It was going to make taking a trip to the storage facility a necessary next step.

"Eliot, do you work tonight?" I asked when I came back out with my new clothes on.

"No, I have the night off and told Hildy if she needed me, she should find someone else to help her."

Okay then.

"Dani, do you have time to go to the storage unit before hanging out with Ian? Should we call him to go with us? He offered to help, but I want your take on how much he's involved."

"He was helpful last time," she said, then sighed. "But I'm just not sure if we need four sets of hands in this pot."

"There's no reason we shouldn't be done before your date. But you can leave from there if we run long." Eliot and I could handle a storage unit by ourselves after the three of us took a first glance.

"Got it. Then you could make the storage unit thing into a date." She smiled that mischievous smile, and I rolled my eyes.

I wasn't against it, but there was a possibility we might need her help if something came up there that involved her mom. We could always call her back if that happened.

"We'll play it by ear."

"Fair enough." She smiled. "Do you need to go home

though? Maybe take a shower to get the milkshake out of your hair?"

I patted my hair frantically. I had been sure everything was wiped off, but I encountered a blob that I had not in fact cleaned up, and it made me groan. "Thanks for telling me now. How about we meet up at the storage unit in forty-five minutes? According to the website, the office is open until six. I have a feeling we're going to need their help to even get to the storage unit since they don't typically just let you in without a code."

"Sounds like a plan," Dani said, pushing me out of the way so that she could escape to her car.

"How are we going to get into the storage unit?" I asked Eliot as we both watched Dani get in her car and speed off two seconds later.

"I have some ideas. Why don't you go shower, and then we'll meet back up?" He leaned on the cash register counter with his arms and ankles crossed. "I've dealt with a lot of families who had to come to terms with a relative doing bad things. She seems totally unfazed by all this even though her mom might be the prime suspect. Is that normal?"

"Define normal."

He chuckled. "Normal for her?"

"Yes and no. She grew up in a very volatile household."

"I get that." He rubbed his chin with a broad hand. "If it really is her mom, do you think she'll be okay?"

"Define okay." I shook my head. "I think she'll deal with whatever comes up as best she can. I will be there for her if things fall apart. We've done that for each other since we were little, so I can handle it."

He reached out and took my hand from where it was tucked around my waist and then brought it to his lips. I felt the brush of skin against skin all the way to my toes.

"You're a good egg, Jax Tapman. She knows it. I know it. The whole world knows it, and we'll figure this out because that's what good eggs do."

Who knew you could go all melty at being called an egg?

CHAPTER FIFTEEN

I was both curious and hesitant as we pulled up at the front gate of the storage facility. How would we get in? Surely there were laws, or at least rules, that the front desk would have to follow since we didn't have a code to get through the gate, never mind that the unit didn't belong to us even if we did have the key.

I let Eliot be the first to go in and then Dani, me bringing up the rear and hoping things wouldn't go sideways before we got a chance to use the key.

There was already someone standing at the front desk doing business, so I took a seat in front of the windows and waited.

"Figure it out, Seth," the irate woman said. "You can't just sell a storage unit out from underneath someone who hasn't been given notification that it's up for clearing out." She tugged her purple blazer around her and flipped her black hair over her shoulder.

"I'm telling you the letters went out. Three in a row, three months in a row, and that unit was sold two weeks ago. If you wanted it, you should have paid the rent like everyone else does, and then there wouldn't have been any reason for me to send it to auction."

She stamped her foot, and I wondered if she thought that was going to get her anything. For one, Seth couldn't see it, and for two, even if he could, I highly doubted he would be moved by a three-year-old tantrum, but that was just me.

"There were things in there!" She was verging on yelling, and though I was sure she was frustrated, there didn't appear to be anything Seth could do. Poor guy.

"Unit 447 is no longer yours, Mrs. Thomas, and before you ask again, no, I cannot tell you who won it in the auction. That's against our policy. I'm not breaking it for anyone. If that answers all your questions, then you can go ahead and go. I don't have anything else I can give you. And the code you use for the gate has been changed, so unless you get another unit, you can no longer enter the yard."

She huffed and puffed, but she did not blow his opinion in a different direction.

She did, however, stomp out of the office with a glare that should have been able to crystallize the glass door in front of her. Instead, she tried to slam it, but it was on an automatic compression arm and swung in, so it took quite some time to actually close. The four of us watched every second of her seething. I didn't hear what she said as she stalked to her car, but whatever it was nearly turned the air blue.

I gave us all a moment to recover by just sitting in my chair and waiting for Seth to call me up to the desk. He might need a minute to decompress, and since I was about to ask him to open the gate for me, even though I didn't have a unit, I was willing to wait until he was mentally in a better place.

"You good?" Eliot asked about two seconds before I had been ready to open my mouth.

Seth blew out a sigh and then pulled his ball cap off and put it back on while clearing his throat. "Sorry about that. This is the third time we've had to shut down her access to the unit. The first two times she was able to save herself by paying at the very last minute but this time she never even called. I don't make the decisions, the owners do, so there wouldn't have been anything I could do for her regardless."

"That's rough."

"Yeah, and she was my first customer of the day since my shift just started. Margo and Tim are on vacation for the week, and I feel like things are jumping without them on site. Maybe it can only go up from here? Sorry." He said it with a weak smile that came off as very uncomfortable.

"No need to apologize," I said. "We get it. Owning a diner gives us a very unique perspective on dealing with customers, so you don't have to go down into why that happened." I paused because it occurred to me this information might be something we could use. "Unless you need to vent."

"I don't want to take up all your time. I'm sure you have other things to do. And I know you don't have a unit at this facility, Jax, so if you're going to ask me to do something I shouldn't be doing in aid to your investigation, I can't, even if I would want to. I need this job."

He used his fingers to air quote around investigation. What were we going to do now?

"It's me that we're here for," Eliot said. "Hildy asked me to come down and pull a few things out and gave me her code. I had just wanted to let you know I was going in under her number in case you saw me on camera and knew I wasn't a usual in the yard."

I stared at Eliot in disbelief. When did Hildy get a storage unit here? I'd have to wait to get any answers until later because, at the moment, Seth was doffing his hat again and thanking Eliot for giving him a warning. Apparently, strange things had been happening around here lately. Which meant they were keeping a much closer eye on who went in and out.

My brain immediately focused in on the fact that if they had footage of the front gate, and we could see who had gone in and match that up with who had sat fiddling with my jukebox at table three in the diner, we'd have a name and an identity. But first we had to get in, and then I had to ask Eliot how he'd managed to get Hildy's code from her when I didn't even know she'd had a storage unit here.

Dani had been on her phone this whole time, so she hadn't been much help but also hadn't been a hindrance, so that counted for something. But I still called her out once we all piled into Eliot's car, leaving her car in the parking lot for when it was time for her date with Ian.

"Hey there, screen rat, what's up with that?" I asked, turning in my seat and pulling the belt out so that it couldn't choke me.

"Maybe you don't remember, but Seth and I dated for a while, and he was not happy when I told him it wasn't going to work between us. We didn't seem to want the same things." She set her phone down on her thigh. "I thought it might be better if I stayed out of the way with the conversation instead of being the one to ask him for things and have him push back just because. Besides, Eliot had it handled and had a far better story than either of us." She tapped him on the shoulder. "But when did Hildy get a unit here, and how did you know to ask?"

"Define get a unit."

I couldn't help it—I laughed way more than I should have. He ignored me as he input the code on the keypad, but I could see his smile in the side view mirror. I wasn't afraid to admit it made me feel all warm and fuzzy inside.

"So whose unit is it actually?" I asked as soon as we were

through the gate.

"It's not a unit at all. She has a trailer she doesn't want parked at the restaurant for when we do catering events. To her, it's an eye sore even though it's beautifully decked out and has her logo across both sides. She just doesn't want it in the parking lot or at her house."

I gave him the side eye. That was very convenient. And then it hit me.

"And when exactly did this trailer move here?"

I watched, enchanted, as a blush creeped from his ears to his cheeks and down his neck. He mumbled something that I was pretty sure I caught but wanted to be absolutely certain.

"When did you say she got an account here?"

"About an hour ago. We're going to move the trailer tomorrow."

"Why am I not surprised?"

He had the grace to look a little sheepish while Dani just laughed.

"You're useful to have around," she said. "Are you sure you don't want to defect and come over to the light side of working in a diner and slinging hash? We can't promise top of the line lobster flown in from Maine, but I bet we're a whole lot more fun with pancakes. And you could make sure Jax never again gets teased for burning toast. Just saying."

Fortunately, by this time, we had pulled up to the rolling door of the storage unit we were looking for according to the three numbers on the key, and I got out before anyone else could say anything.

It looked innocuous enough, no bent doors or chisel marks. The lock appeared intact, and the concrete lip beneath the door didn't appear to have any scuff marks on it. It was pristine, which could be an indicator all its own if someone had done a bad deed and then scrubbed the place clean.

I might want to consider more fully laying off the true crime shows…

Since I had the key, I took it out of my pocket once Dani and Eliot were stationed behind me.

I wasn't entirely certain what I thought I would find within, but I can tell you very clearly it was not a scrawled message in the same orange crayon. The words *Loans Lies Lessons Learned* covered a piece of large paper attached to a beveled mirror on a vanity that looked like it was from the nineteen-thirties. It sat at the very front of the nearly empty ten-by-twenty unit. Right next to it was a mannequin that seemed to ping a memory in the back of my mind and several storage bins marked for the holidays but not much else. I felt like we were being led on a merry chase, except this was anything but merry, and I might as well be chasing my own tail.

For his part, Eliot walked into the unit then ran his gloved hand over the writing—where had he come up with those?—and then stood back with a grimace on his face.

"This is all so confusing," he said. "Why lead us here for nothing? They could have put this on the order slip instead of pulling us over to a storage facility." Walking into the unit, he poked at the mannequin and then took the lid off one of the decoration boxes.

"Anything weird?" I asked.

"Not unless you think this Rudolph is a little strange." He produced a neon-green reindeer with a psychedelic rainbow swirl nose.

"Well, yes, I don't know how someone wouldn't consider that strange." But I again got the brain ping. "Where have I seen these things before?"

"They're my mom's," Dani said and then crumpled to the asphalt right outside the unit. Dang it.

Eliot and I stared at each other for a split second before I knelt next to my best friend. "This doesn't mean anything. It doesn't have to mean anything at all. Someone could just be trying to blackmail her. We talked about this."

She drew in a sharp breath. "I know that, Jax, but I also know that the mannequin hasn't been in our house for years, and the vanity was my grandmother's. My mom told me I wasn't going to have it passed down to me because it was ruined and that she'd put it in the trash."

Yikes. "Maybe she put it out to the curb, and someone picked it up. You know how people around here stop for any garage sales, thrift stores, and especially roadside freebies."

"But it's not ruined." She rested her forehead on her bent knees and blew out a big breath.

I looked up at Eliot and felt so helpless. What if it really was Nancy and someone had gotten her storage key? Why would she hide all her things in here after saying she had gotten rid of them?

"Do you think Seth might let us look at the footage of the facility so that we can see if anyone came to this unit recently?" I asked Eliot.

"It might at least be worth a try."

"Any idea how are we going to explain that we're at a completely different area than we should be?" I said the words while stroking Dani's hair. She blew out another big breath.

"We tell him I'm here to check in on my mom's unit and that she gave me the key," Dani said. She raised her head from her knees and a look of determination came across her face, the one that told anyone and everyone that she meant business.

Rising from the pavement, she dusted her rear end off and then thrust her chin into the air. "Eliot, if you wouldn't mind staying here, just in case anyone else comes by, I'd appreciate it. Jax, you're with me."

Then Dani dragged me down the alley to the end of the building even though I was very clearly walking as fast as I could.

"You okay?" I asked.

"I have nothing to say until I get some more information." She pulled her phone from her little backpack and sent out a call while we walked. Whoever it was answered on the first ring. "Are you aware of a storage unit?"

Her stepdad? Most likely not her mom…

"Okay, thank you." And she hung up. But I didn't have a chance to ask for any more information because she whipped that front office door open and marched up to the front desk like a Valkyrie on a mission.

Unfortunately, Seth was not at his post. Even more unfortunately, there was a service bell on the front desk that she started pinging like she was on turbo mode.

I laid my hand over hers after about the fortieth ding. I wanted to say the words I was supposed to, but man, was my brain stumbling over itself to come up with some explanation that was different than what we'd seen. Was the note-writer leading us to a storage unit of Nancy's things so that we'd look at her harder? Take her more seriously as a suspect for this murder? Were they pointing to the lies she had told Dani to make us doubt everything Nancy had told us?

I remembered the mannequin now. Dani's mom had once proudly displayed it in a craft room. Nancy always had some kind of glamorous dress on the thing and decorated it for every holiday. I hadn't been inside Dani's childhood home for many, many years, so I had no idea when things had been moved out, but we'd get to that later.

Dani had slipped her hand out from under mine while I was off in my head and was now dinging the bell obsessively again.

I heard someone pounding down the stairs to the left and figured Seth had finally heard Dani's call.

He emerged from the stairwell and threw a very mad-dog look in our general direction. Did it have something to do with the fact that his once-pristine shirt was now absolutely covered in some black substance?

Part of me did not want to dare ask what had happened, and the other part, that nosy part I was very aware couldn't live without knowing all the deets, had to ask.

"Did you have a run-in with an octopus?" I asked.

"No. I need a freaking new job!"

"Okay." I dragged out the word as he lumbered over to his post behind the desk, shaking his head.

He snorted as he looked down at his sooty hands. He had a fine dust all over him that I could now see looked a lot like toner.

"Should I even ask what happened?" I had an idea it had something to do with the printer, which I could now hear beeping, and the toner cartridge next to it. I hadn't seen one of those in years.

"I have a feeling you're here for something else, so just tell me what you need, and I'll get it before I finish dousing myself in soap and water. Maybe a little alcohol, though the kind might be up for debate."

I didn't want to laugh because he looked so down in the dumps, but I couldn't help it. Even Dani, in her Valkyrie mode, couldn't help herself. And then he laughed with us. It was edged with some sarcasm, but the tone of the room changed.

"We can wait until you're cleaned up if you need us to," Dani said, her elevated anger floating back into the realm of calm I was more used to. "I'm looking for some footage of who has been in and out of here for the last few days. There's a question I have about a unit, and we're trying to figure out who's been there."

"Does this have anything to do with finding out who killed June?" he asked.

I hated to lie, but I wasn't sure if saying yes would then cut the legs out from under Dani's story about her mom's unit.

"Because if it has to do with finding out who killed my great-aunt June then I'm willing to look the other way. But if it's just a unit question, legally I have to say no due to our rules regarding privacy." He kept constant eye contact with me, and I had a decision to make.

But Dani made it before I could.

"Let's get down to brass tacks here, then, Seth. The unit appears to be my mom's. My stepdad was unaware there was one, but we were left a key at the diner that opens the unit. I would like to know if she's been in there recently. There was also a message on an old vanity that was written in the same crayon that was on a note we got at the diner. I want answers regarding my mom, no matter what they are. You want answers for your great-aunt because her death was way too early. Let us see the footage, and maybe we can both get closure on this."

He didn't move for a full fifteen seconds as he and Dani stared at each other. I counted while holding my breath.

Time for me to jump in, just in case he was considering saying no, because he and Dani had not lasted beyond a few dates. "If you can give us the link or whatever we have to do to get access to the cameras, we'd appreciate it," I said. "And then you can go get cleaned up. I've heard that the alcohol you talked about earlier can also take toner out of the shirt without ruining it. My mom used it all the time when I was going through my 'I must be an artist' phase."

Finally, he broke his stare-down with Dani and glanced at me. "Funny, I had one of those too. My mom always used turpentine, but it ruined everything." He pulled his shirt away from his stomach. It wasn't good. "I have a feeling I'm going to just have to trash it."

"I'm sorry," Dani said.

"Not your fault." He blew out a breath. "Normally, I would need you to get some kind of warrant to be able to see the footage, so let's just say I left the program open while I went to go get cleaned up, and you happened to see it. If you find anything your dad might be able to use, Jax, he'll need to go through the process of getting a warrant, but at least you'll know whether or not it's worth going to all that trouble."

Excellent!

CHAPTER SIXTEEN

Dani and I stood there patiently on the other side of the desk as Seth leaned over the computer. He went to put his fingers on the keys but then realized how dirty he really was. Instead, he grabbed a pen out of the cup next to the keyboard, typed in a few commands, and then up popped the video. Holy cow. I could see Eliot standing outside the storage unit. The picture was a little grainy and the colors slightly off, but I would know that face and stature anywhere.

We were in business!

"Enjoy," Seth said. He left the computer and disappeared back through the door right off the main room. All I saw were steps and wondered if he lived above the office.

I wasted no time sitting down and scrolling through the videos. At first, I had no idea what I was doing. However, I was able to get the small arrows at the bottom to work after a few tries. I went back four days, hoping that would be good enough. Unfortunately, the video flipped back and forth between the different cameras every few seconds, so it was hard to get any real idea of what was going on. Eventually, I did get the hang of the flip and found a rhythm where I could tell when the aisle with Dani's mom's storage unit would come up. Dani stood behind me with her hand gripping my shoulder.

I squealed, like for real squealed, and then smiled up at Dani when I came across someone walking *by the unit*. There was no car in sight, which put my sleuthing antennae up. But they didn't stop at the unit, so bust on that one. We kept watching though, and the same person appeared again and again.

"They keep coming back by. That's three times now. He's wearing headphones and has a steady pace to his walk. Do you think maybe he's just using the storage unit's quiet alleys as a walking course?" I asked.

"My neighbor does that," Dani said. "She says it's much

safer because there's hardly anyone here, and since she has a key and pays the fees, she might as well get some additional benefits for her buck."

"Okay, so we'll chalk this up to someone who loves their exercise. Moving on."

To say the footage so far was disappointing was a bit of an understatement. But the next time I saw someone come by, they did stop, and I wondered if there was a way to zoom in. Because not only did they stop, they also used a key to open the padlock and then raise the door. In fact, they went in and stayed for a few minutes. I didn't fast forward there at all, but I did note the time on a sticky. Yesterday at eleven.

Could this be the person who brought the key to my diner and put it into the jukebox?

I paused and turned to Dani. "We found the key today because of the note on the Spy Spindle, but do you think it was placed there today? I mean, it could have been there earlier and the person was getting tired of us not finding it. Maybe they wrote the note and stuck it on the Spy Spindle to lead us in the right direction today even though the key had already been there?"

"I don't know if there's a way to tell that," Dani said. "But I had just cleaned the jukeboxes yesterday afternoon. I even pulled the glass off and swiped under the mount. I can't imagine that the envelope wouldn't have fallen out at some point with how I was cleaning it."

There went that theory. "All right, something to keep in mind then. But the person could have still gone to the unit yesterday and then delivered the key today."

"Absolutely, let's keep looking."

I couldn't tell anything about the person other than that whoever it was appeared to be shorter than me and walked a little slow, though that could have been their way of being stealthy.

I marked the time and let the video play again as they left in a compact car.

A few minutes later, another car came on the scene and rushed past the unit then jerked to a halt, leaving only the taillight of the car hanging in the picture. This person was taller and more svelte than the first person as he approached the unit. He turned sideways and almost looked at the camera, but then whipped his head back around to the front, and I lost the chance to see his face. It was definitely a guy from the way he was built.

Whoever it was ducked down and tried to shove something under the door. But I was pretty sure that door was hard pressed against the concrete floor. How else would they save items inside from any kind of flooding? He stood back up and shook his head.

"Turn just a bit. Just a little bit. Please." Dani gripped my shoulder harder, digging her nails in.

I waited a few more seconds to see what he'd do. The answer was nothing, just stood there like he wasn't sure what came next.

"And then he turned!" I said out loud as he did just that. "Woohoo!" Yet it didn't help me very much. Even though he turned, I had no idea who he was. He wore a hunter-green beanie, which meant I couldn't see if he had hair or what color it was if he did. And the camera wasn't as sharply focused as I would have liked. I had been able to recognize Eliot right off the bat because I knew his face by heart. This guy could have been someone I had seen around town, but I wasn't able to identify him due to the angle and quality of the picture.

"Any chance you recognize him?" I asked Dani. "Because I'm not seeing anything distinctive."

"Maybe that's the whole point," she said.

I let the video play a while longer, and the guy got back in his car and left without ever having accessed the unit.

After another thirty minutes, during which I skipped through as much as I could, another person walked up to the unit. This one in a turquoise jogging suit. My heart sank, and Dani's grip tightened then released.

"Nancy."

Dani's mom bent to the lock, pulled a key out of her pocket, worked it into the lock, toggled it back and forth, and then opened the unit. She strolled in empty-handed and then right back out about five minutes later, still not carrying anything. Was this really her storage unit? Who was the person who accessed it before her and the one who couldn't?

"Can we turn it off for a few minutes?" Dani asked as she sank into a chair on the other side of the counter. She was framed in the sunlight pouring through the big window so that her face and expression were in a kind of shadow, but I didn't miss the way her voice sounded like she was holding back tears.

"What do you want to do?" I asked quietly. Just because Nancy owned a key to the unit didn't mean she had actually killed

June. "I have a hard time believing she would have put a note on the vanity. And she's never even been in the diner the whole time we've owned it, so how could she have put the note in the jukebox?"

What did the person who gave us the note and the key want us to find out? I felt more confused than before we had started this. Were they friend or foe of Nancy?

"I don't really know," Dani said in a very flat and measured voice. "Herbert had no idea about the storage unit, and I can't imagine my mother trying to put clues into her own storage unit for us to find. Why wouldn't she just tell me?"

"Unless maybe she thinks we're not doing enough and she wants to move us along a different path?"

"Again, I don't know." Dani sighed. "All I do know is that I need to get out of here. If you want to watch the rest of the footage to see if someone else comes in and has access to her storage unit, I'll leave you to it. I need fresh air."

"I can do that later." I marked down the time stamp on the video so that I could pick it back up as soon as I got Dani out of here. Nothing was more important than her well-being.

We left the office then came to the edge of the last building and were about to move toward the gate when someone shouted Dani's name, and we both turned abruptly,

It was Ian. He opened his arms, and Dani ran at him full bore.

Once she was in his arms, he stroked her hair, and she looked up at him as if he could save the whole world with one smile. Maybe he could do that for her world. She deserved some comfort after everything we'd endured this afternoon.

"Have you been here long?" I asked.

Dani tucked her head back under his chin, and I knew how comforting that could be in a moment of crisis. I'd done the same thing with Eliot. It had made everything okay, if only for a moment.

"About two hours. I'm trying to organize what I brought with me when I moved here. I want to see if I can whittle it down now that I'm settled. If I haven't used it in the last three months, then maybe I don't need it?"

Smart. Resourceful. Good answer.

"This might seem like a weird question, but did you happen to see anyone three rows down messing with a storage unit?" I asked.

"More investigating?" He hooked an arm around Dani's

waist when she finally let go of him.

"Something like that. A clue was left at the diner, and we were here just to see what it meant."

"I did see someone drive around the facility a few times, actually. I wasn't sure if maybe he just couldn't find his unit. He was driving a compact car, but I never saw where he stopped."

"Was he wearing a green beanie?"

He closed his eyes for a few seconds. "Not green. More of a dark blue."

It could have been the color distortion from the monitors that I'd recognized when looking at Eliot!

"Would you be able to identify him if you saw him again?"

He shrugged and Dani held on tighter. "Probably not. I glanced at him when he drove around the third time, but I can only say for certain that he was a guy and looked like he might be tall with the way he was scrunched into the little car."

"That's something at least. Thanks."

"Are you going back to the office now?" Dani cuddled closer into Ian's chest.

"If you want to hang with Ian, I can run back and do that myself."

"You don't mind, Jax?"

"Of course not. Take the time you need. I'll swing back by when I'm done with Seth, and then we can make a plan from there."

"Okay." She took Ian's hand and led him over to his car and storage unit.

I didn't quite run back to the office, but it was a close thing. When I got there, Seth was just coming down the stairs again. This time in a much cleaner shirt.

"All better?" I asked as I sat in his chair again.

"Much, thanks. You find anything?"

"I might have. There was a man who tried to put something in the storage unit Dani's looking at, but I don't recognize him. Is he someone you've seen before?" I scrolled back through the footage, past Nancy going in and out of the unit, and paused on the image of the man in the beanie when he looked at the camera.

I watched Seth's expression to see if he had any reaction to the image, but he just squinted and seemed to be studying the picture intently.

Finally, he shook his head. "No, I wish I did, but I don't. However, I can look to see whose entry code he used to get in if you don't mind me taking my chair back."

I quickly moved out of the way and then waved him into his chair.

With a few clicks, he pulled up a long string of data on the computer that I did not understand. But I didn't have to, as long as he did.

"Huh." He sat back in the office chair and crossed his arms over his chest.

I waited a few seconds, not wanting to push him, but I didn't win that fight. "What's huh?"

"Well, he used the master code. There aren't many people who have access to that. Usually just me and the owners. There are probably a few others who have it, but it's not typical for anyone to not have their own code." He pressed a few more keys but then shook his head. "Yeah, I'm not sure who that is. I could try calling Margo at the resort. She should know anyone who would be able to access the facility with that code. It would almost have to be someone she knows."

"I would really appreciate that." I turned and looked out the window so that I wasn't staring at him while he dialed his boss. That didn't mean I wasn't listening.

"Yeah, Margo, I have a coded entry with the master pass this morning. A guy, kind of tall, wearing a beanie." He was silent for a little bit, and I was about to come unglued waiting for an answer.

"Yeah, no, it's definitely not Shelby. Okay, I'll rekey it. Thanks. See you soon." And he hung up.

He put the phone back down on the desk and tapped a few more keys before turning to me. I was dying to hear whatever she'd said.

I didn't have to wait too much longer.

"So Margo says that her sister Shelby is in town and that she just gave her the code the day before yesterday. Maybe she knows this guy? I can give you her number if you want."

Oh boy did I ever want!

CHAPTER SEVENTEEN

———

"I think I have a lead," I said as I trotted around the corner and approached the storage unit where I'd left Eliot. It felt like it had been at least three hours since I'd walked away, but in reality, it was probably no more than forty-five minutes.

Ian and Dani were standing with him in the open unit, and they all turned to me as I came even with them. Good. This way I wouldn't have to repeat the story over and over again.

"That guy we saw in the video used a master code to get through the gate. Seth called his boss on vacation and learned the only person who has the number besides Seth and the owners is a sister. Seth reset the code, and he gave me the sister's phone number to see if she shared the code with anyone." I was nearly giddy at the end of my little speech, and I wasn't alone. Dani grabbed my hands and squeezed.

"That is awesome. Did you try calling her?"

"Not yet. I wanted to come talk to you all before I did anything else. Eliot's request…"

"Go ahead and do it now, then," he said.

I carefully hit the numbers on my cell phone and waited four rings before the voicemail picked up. I raised my eyebrows and shrugged my shoulders at the three standing in front of me.

"Just say you need to get in touch with her and that her sister gave you the number," Dani said.

I did just that but then felt a little deflated. I had really hoped she would answer and give us all the information about whoever this guy was so that we could go find out what he wanted with a storage unit filled with Dani's mom's stuff.

Speaking of that, I had been thinking about how to address the subject, and now was as good a time as any.

"Was there anything else in the unit?" I asked to ease into what I knew was probably not going to be a welcome request.

"Nothing that would give us any new information." Eliot gestured at the contents behind him. "Nothing any stranger than that Rudolph in all of the bins, and the boxes also just held memorabilia that would normally be stashed in the attic of anyone's house."

"Your parents have an attic, Dani. Did Herbert say anything else about the storage unit?"

Her smile faded a little, and she stepped closer to Ian. "He said he had no idea she had one, and then he hung up."

I sighed. "I think we're going to have to talk with him."

"I had a feeling you were going to say that."

"Do we have time before your hang-out session tonight?"

"I'm open to whatever time." Ian took Dani's hand and kissed the back of her knuckles. "Why don't you get this over with, and then your mind might be clearer, and you can relax with me after?"

"Okay, that might help."

I appreciated that more than I could say. I didn't want to wait, but I also hadn't wanted to cut off her plans in pursuit of a killer, even if it would hopefully clear her mom's name. We had signs pointing to Nancy, but I was still holding on to the hope that it was someone else. I just needed to figure out who. And this guy from the video was a good place to start. On that front, though, we couldn't do anything else but wait for Shelby to call me back. If we could at least clear up things with Dani's stepdad, it might be a good in-between step.

Eliot ushered everyone out of the unit and then rolled down the door behind us. "I'll go home and see if I can finally get in touch with Mildred. You want to meet up afterward, Jax?"

"Yeah. Yeah, I do." I kissed him on the cheek before he left to his car.

With everyone set on their course, we divided up. I had taken the key after Eliot had snapped the padlock closed, and it was safely stowed in my pocket. Dani and I stopped in at the front desk to talk to Seth briefly before we left. He agreed to let us know if he saw anyone hovering near Dani's mom's unit.

Technically, we didn't know if that was only Nancy's unit since she wasn't the only one with a key to it, but we stuck with that story for the moment, just in case. I had considered asking Seth to verify who the owner of the unit was, but if it wasn't Nancy, we would have given away that we shouldn't have been in the unit in the first place.

Oh, the tangled webs we weave...

"Do you want to call your mom or stepdad to see where they are before we just head over to the house?" I buckled into her little SUV and took my notebook out of my backpack to jot down some notes about the guy with the beanie and what had been in the storage unit. I didn't want to forget anything.

Much like when we were in my mom's driveway, Dani also waited until I was done writing before putting her car in reverse. She was able to write in the car without getting motion sickness, but I was not. Thankfully, she remembered.

"I'm thinking we should just show up. Catching them off guard might work in our favor, especially since I want to do this before I chicken out. I don't like confrontation of any kind, but I absolutely dread what could happen when we go there and ask about a storage unit full of my mother's things that my stepfather knows nothing about."

Yeah, I had thought about that too, but we needed to at least know who else had a key to the unit, and I really wanted to see if we could get our hands on Nancy's cell phone. Two birds with one stone might be painful, but then at least it would be done.

Dani's phone pinged through the Wi-Fi connection in the car and then a mechanical voice said, "Text from Momzilla."

"Oh, when did you change that?" I asked with a snicker.

"Yesterday," she said, then raised her voice. "Read text."

There was a pause, and then the mechanical voice rang through the car. "Note left on car. Someone threatening me. Drop whatever you're doing and get here. Now."

Once the message ended, we both sat in stunned silence. Fortunately, Dani had not yet moved out of the parking lot at the storage place, she had only backed up and pulled forward to the stop sign before entering traffic. Instead of going forward, she returned the car to its original parking space and rested her wrists on the top of the steering wheel.

"Sounds like we have an open invitation now," I said, making another note in my book.

"But seriously, what is it with these people and leaving notes on cars? Don't they know it could be blown away by a stiff wind or that someone could take it just because they wanted to?" She blew out a breath and then put the car back in reverse once I'd closed my notebook on my lap.

"I don't know. Maybe it's because it's less traceable? A text would tell you who it's coming from."

"Unless you had a burner phone like that lady who called herself Karen and told you about that first key in the back of the jukebox." She checked both ways and then turned right to head to her mother's house.

"There is that."

Dani tapped the steering wheel in a rhythm that didn't match the pop music coming through the speakers.

"Spill it. What's going on in that mind of yours?"

"I just…I mean…" She sighed. "I'm nervous that we have the right person directly in front of us, and I'm doing everything I can to look past her for someone else."

Yeah, great minds sometimes thought alike. But that wasn't what she needed to hear right now. "We have a lot of leads to a lot of things, and it makes sense to not narrow down on any one person and get so caught up in proving that one person did it while not taking all the facts into account."

She turned her head slightly and gave me a small smile. "You sound just like your dad."

"Yeah, he recently told me that he always thought I'd follow in his footsteps and join the police force. But when he saw how much I loved the diner and how much I wanted to run it with you, he backed off from encouraging me in the cop direction."

"Wow! I don't know if I could see you as a cop. Doing all that 'following the rules' stuff seems out of your realm." And she laughed, which meant my whole purpose was served.

Especially since we had just pulled up to the curb at Nancy's house.

"Brace yourself." I unbuckled my seatbelt and grabbed the door handle. "We'll get through this. We just need to get the phone, find out the threat, maybe see if we can get her to say something about the storage unit. If it's gets too heavy in there, we can always leave."

"I'm ready." She unbuckled her own seat belt and turned to me. "Thank you for being here with me."

"Always. Now it's showtime."

Getting out of the car, I tried to remember what the inside of Dani's childhood home looked like. I had almost never come here, and even when I did, I would stay out on the doorstep waiting for Dani to come out to me. Her mom did not like visitors, and her stepdad went along with whatever Nancy said.

I stood next to Dani as she knocked, and yes, you read that right—she had to knock at her own parents' home. It seemed to take forever for anyone to come to the door.

"I thought she said to drop everything and get right over here. *Now*, if I heard her correctly. I'm pretty sure I couldn't have messed that up."

"She did." She knocked again, harder this time.

"Do you think something happened? Should we be checking the windows to make sure everyone is okay? You don't think whoever wrote the note already came by, do you?"

She banged on the door this time.

And finally, it opened. Nancy stood on the threshold of the house with her hair up in curlers and some sort of facial mask covering her from her forehead to the neckline of her designer shell blouse. She did not look pleased to be interrupted in her beauty routine, but she was the one who had demanded we come by. Where was she going all dressed up like that, and who did a facial in the afternoon?

Something felt off here, but I didn't know what it could be.

"Come in already. I don't want the neighbors to see you standing on the stoop. You know better than that. I don't need anyone telling me that I left my only child out of the house."

Right. Because, according to Nancy, she was the very best mother in the whole world, as she would inform anyone who even breathed in her direction. And it was Dani's job to pretend that was true, no matter how very untrue it was.

Dani chose not to fight this time, and I completely understood. We wouldn't get anywhere if we started out with harsh words.

I let Dani go in first. As I entered the house, I could have sworn we'd been thrown back to the eighties. The furniture was brown and tan with waterwheels on it, hewn from fake particle board and the fabric a brushed velvet. There was an honest to goodness wagon-wheel coffee table in the middle of the living room. I skirted around it and settled into the couch that had seen better days. Out came my notepad as I waited for Dani to get this show started.

"Well, at least you finally showed up. I was starting to think you'd decided to cancel on me. Who cares if your own mother gets thrown under the bus?"

"Mom, we're not going to do this. I'm here to help. I came

over as soon as I could. Now where is the note you got so that I can see what it says." She held her hand out, and Nancy scowled at her.

"You don't believe me? You think I'm making up the threat against me just to get some sympathy?"

I honestly had not considered that possibility, but I wasn't completely convinced she wouldn't have done just that.

But then she did produce the note from the front pocket of her knee-length, jean skirt. Dani brought it over to the couch so that we could read it together. Nancy hovered around the edges, pacing back and forth around the coffee table, forcing us to move our feet every time she came between the couch and the coffee table. I literally had to bite my tongue to keep from telling her to go somewhere else.

Glancing at Dani, I saw her eyes had narrowed almost to slits, so I discreetly nudged her with my elbow before taking the note out of her hand and opening it.

A burst of laughter almost escaped my mouth when I saw that someone had gone to a lot of trouble to make the note out of letters cut from a magazine. Actually, when I looked at it closer, it appeared as if they had used some kind of paint program on their computer to put the letters together into words and then printed the whole thing out.

What it said though took me aback, and I read it again, out loud this time to make sure I wasn't reading it wrong.

"*I know you did it. I have proof, plus my own sight as I saw you plunge that knife into that woman's back. Either fall back in line where you belong or the consequences will be dire, and I will tell everyone how truly horrible you are and always have been.*"

Ouch.

"I'm sorry, Mom. That's a terrible note. You must have really taken it hard because it's so scary and mean."

"Don't pretend to care, Danielle Michelle. We both know you don't do anything that doesn't benefit you. You wouldn't even be here to help me if it wasn't going to make you look good to help find another killer."

Dani stiffened next to me, her body vibrating enough to shake the couch. I laid a hand on her wrist, hoping to bring her back to the here and now. It would not help for her to go off against her mom right now

"Steady." I said the word quietly, hoping Dani alone would

hear me.

She didn't relax from her rendition of a frozen banana, but at least she stopped vibrating. That was good since her mother had braced her hand on the back of the couch and would have felt Dani nearing meltdown.

Dani took one long and slow breath and then snapped out of wherever she had been for the moment.

"I'm not doing this for any kind of fame, and I'm not doing this because I don't have anything better to do. I'm doing this for justice and also because I believe you are not the killer. I want to help you, not for any kudos or pats on the back but because it's the right thing to do. But I am not, and I'm going to repeat this louder, I am *not* going to sit here while you insult me."

The two women stared at each other for what felt like forever, and I could not do anything but jump in between them to cut the tension.

"I'm going to take a quick picture of the note, Nancy," I said, trying to redirect the conversation before it devolved into us getting kicked out. "After I do, I urge you to take it to the police. They will probably want to see it, even if it is just from someone trying to blackmail you."

I was fully aware her anger was about to come my way, and I was fine with that. Not to mention, if I got her riled up, I might be able to get her to say something she didn't mean to let slip.

"You might get special treatment because your daddy's a cop, but the rest of us don't, so I don't want to hear it from you. Take your pictures and take the note yourself. I'm going to go do my hair. I have important things planned for this evening."

Of course she did.

As soon as she left the room, I waved Dani over to where Nancy's cell phone was resting on the arm of the couch opposite me. "Quickly," I whispered.

I tried to keep an eye on the hallway while using my own cell phone to take a few pictures of the note. Nancy's whole head had been covered in those plastic, pink snap-together curlers, so I knew we had a little time, but I was still watching just in case.

"Anything?" I whispered to Dani.

"We're lucky she never set up her phone to need a password to unlock. I'm looking through the texts right now. She is in a heated battle with Mrs. Jeffries down the street about her music, and her meds just got refilled and are ready to be picked up." She hummed as she kept scrolling. "Oh, Herbert forgot to get the right kind of creamer yesterday, and her library books are overdue. I'm sure she's going to have a field day with the library staff on that one."

"Nothing else?" Part of me wanted to join her across the room and look at the texts over her shoulder. The other part knew that if Nancy came down the hall, and we quickly broke apart while trying to hide that we were looking at her phone, it would be worse than if I stayed on the couch and could distract her again. I was completely confident Dani would get all the info anyway. I just wanted in on the discovery. She grabbed her own phone and took a picture of whatever was currently on the screen.

And then her eyes widened as she kept scrolling, and she opened her mouth in a gasp. "June's on here, and it's nasty."

Breaking my own best practice, I scrambled out of my seat and looked over her shoulder. Dani scrolled up through many messages, all in caps. There were threats and warnings, all from Nancy. June's responses were just a bunch of smiley face emojis.

"The last one is from about an hour before we saw June dead at the theater, and it's June saying come and get me."

Uh-oh.

CHAPTER EIGHTEEN

We both heard a door slam from down the hallway, and Dani quickly put the phone back where it had been as I resumed my seat on the couch.

We had a lot to discuss as soon as we could get out of here. As far as I was concerned, now was just as good as any other moment to make our exit. But then her stepdad came in through the garage.

Herbert Johnson was short with thinning, silver hair and a paunch. He was the polar opposite of Nancy in that he was nice, incredibly nice, and had a smile for everyone. He was a whole different animal than Dani's dad too.

That smile was very much on show as he saw Dani standing between the couch and the kitchen.

"Oh, it's so good to see you, honey. I didn't know you were stopping by. I would have come in sooner." He wiped his hands on an old rag and then grinned sheepishly. "I'd hug you, but I've been under the hood of your mother's car, and I don't think we want all this grease on you."

She hugged him anyway and kissed him on the cheek. "No problem, Herbert. Mom had an issue she wanted me to look at, so she asked me to come over."

That was not at all how it had actually happened, but I wasn't going to correct her. I knew she had her reasons for the spin she'd put on the non-request.

"She's been going through a lot lately. I know she doesn't always thank you, but I'm sure she appreciates it."

It was like watching a play where everyone knew their lines and said them by rote. It was also the only way things stayed civil for everyone. Nancy was Herbert's sixth wife, and from what I could tell, he did not want to start over again in his seventies with a divorce and making a shift to a whole new life. Plus, he'd been around for years to help raise Dani when Nancy couldn't be bothered. It was one of the few reasons I could think of that would make him stay and endure this kind of marriage.

Speak of the devil, she came down the hallway in her fancy shirt with her hair artfully tousled and her makeup about two degrees too vibrant. Blue eyeshadow was not her best friend, but she wore it anyway.

"I'm out of here," she said, throwing a glittering wrap over her shoulders while she stepped into heels she had waiting at the door. She barely even looked at Herbert and focused solely on Dani. Picking up her purse, she grabbed her phone and tucked it into her neckline under her bra strap. "Take care of what we talked about. And make sure you show this one's dad that I am not the culprit." She jerked her thumb at me then sailed out the door to the garage without saying goodbye.

"Where is she off to?" Dani asked Herbert as soon as we heard the garage door roll up.

"I think it's a salsa class over at the Y. She'll be back later. I have dinner in the crock pot already, so I might take a little nap while the house is quiet."

"We'll get out of your hair then," she said, patting him on the shoulder.

"Not much to get out of." He rubbed his balding head and smiled again. "I hope whatever your mom has you working on will help with figuring out who killed June. A tense wife isn't always the easiest person to deal with."

"Hopefully we have some answers coming soon," I said. Had she told him she was about to become a martyr of shoddy police work?

"Hey, before we go, do have any idea what Mom had against June recently? I know they go back a long way, but they were…exchanging words right before June died. I haven't been able to get Mom to tell me what it was about."

Herbert shook his head and sighed. "She was mad because I had been talking to June about some financial things having to do with retirement and savings. I don't know who else she thought I should be talking to, but you know how your mom can be." He brought his hand up to cover a yawn.

"We'll let you go take your nap, then. I hope you get some good rest."

"I'm going to need it." He chuckled and then walked us to the door. After he patted my shoulder and gave Dani another hug, we were out the door.

Part of me wanted to immediately start yakking about what we'd found and what it could mean, but the other part of me saw that Dani needed a moment. I took her keys out of her hand then opened the passenger side door and waited for her to get in. She laid her head back and closed her eyes, and my heart broke a little more for her.

Before getting in the driver's seat, I texted Eliot and told him we would need a little time before I was ready to unleash Dani on him. He texted back he was available whenever and that, if he thought Stella Luna could open the door, he'd go over now and start making dinner.

I told him where the key was in the front garden, inside a reading frog sitting on a lily pad, and then let him know he had free rein in the kitchen. When he didn't text back right away, I put my phone under my leg in the driver's seat so that I wouldn't be distracted as we moved into the next phase that I knew, without a shadow of a doubt, was coming.

Years ago, when things were tough, I would get her from her house and crank up Evanescence or Offspring to the loudest possible decibel so that her bad thoughts would be drowned out until she was ready to handle them. It worked then, and I had a feeling it would work again now. I had nothing to lose by trying.

I released the parking brake and hit the aux button on the steering wheel so that the phone under my leg would start cycling through the playlist I'd made up years ago and never gotten rid of.

She hugged my arm and then sat back in her seat, humming to the music. She shut her eyes, and a few tears leaked out, so I took the music up to a louder volume without hitting the ceiling of noise. We cruised the ten miles back to my house where Eliot would be waiting, making food and ready to dive head-first into figuring out who was playing tricks, who was doing bad things, and who we had to hand over to my dad on a silver platter of suspect à la mode.

She turned down the volume as I turned onto my street. "Instead of me hanging out with Ian by ourselves, how do you feel about us crashing your dinner here? I have ideas," she said as we pulled to a stop in my driveway next to Eliot's SUV.

I wanted to ask what those ideas were and if they had to do with what she'd found on her mother's phone, but she didn't give me a chance to ask. All of the sudden she rocketed out of the car. Before I could blink, she had opened my front door and waltzed inside. She'd moved so fast I hadn't even had a chance to unhook my seatbelt and get my car door fully open.

Stella Luna did not try to dart out of the door when Dani opened it, but I figured that was because Eliot was in the house, and she would be stuck to his side like rolls to an ungreased pan.

I took my time going in my own house. That would give Dani a moment to let Eliot know there were going to be four for dinner and to text or call Ian to come over.

Yet what to my wondering eyes should appear in the front window but Dani jumping into someone's arms and kissing him like it was the end of a Hallmark movie.

That was why she had bolted out of the car! Ian was here. That made me feel better about our chances of coming to some sort of plan to get to the bottom of this mystery, and that was all good.

As I entered the house at a much slower pace, I kept quiet. Eliot was talking from the kitchen island, and I didn't want to interrupt him.

"So then I made the filet, and I turned to the new sous chef and told him we would never do that again." Eliot laughed. Ian smiled, and Dani giggled. After the atmosphere at Dani's childhood home, this was a very welcomed change.

I was going to let that ride, but then the aromas wafting from my kitchen hit my nose, and I started salivating. "What on earth are you making? It smells absolutely heavenly in here!" I set down my little backpack purse on the island. Stella tried to bat it off the counter, but I moved it out of her way.

"Stew. You had actual food in your refrigerator this time, and I decided to do a stew that I haven't had in years. I don't know how to make it for less than an army, and it's too basic for Hildy's restaurant, so I thought I'd do it here. You've got tons of room for leftovers in that very empty freezer."

He wasn't wrong. I had a small carton of ice cream in there and an empty ice cube tray. I was pretty sure that was it. And then I was certain that was it because Eliot took the time to open the freezer and show how it looked like a barren wasteland.

If there was enough stew left over, I was willing to cram my freezer with as many servings as he'd leave for me. To make the evening even better, I caught a whiff of some sort of bread baking in the oven as he pulled open the door to check the rising loaf. I was positive my kitchen had never smelled this good.

There would have to be more than enough for a week. I could pace myself. Right?

Stella Luna strutted around the island as Eliot came around its corner to sit on one of the three stools I had situated there. The sassy cat completely bypassed me and jumped right into his lap as if she always belonged there.

"How long before dinner's ready?" I asked, putting out my hand to pet Stella Luna. She snapped her gaze to me, but she didn't move or swat at me as I stroked her from head to tail, so we were good for the moment.

"Should be about an hour for maximum flavor. I've let it cook all day before, but this will still be good."

"I don't doubt it. So, since we have an hour, we should get down to sorting out what we learned today and see if any of it adds up or leads us in a new direction." I plopped my trusty notebook on the island.

"I feel unprepared," Ian said and chuckled when Dani also produced a notebook and Eliot removed a smaller version from the back pocket of his pants.

"No worries, we're almost like professional amateurs. Or Jax and I are. Eliot is the real deal." Dani smiled and hugged Ian's arm. "You can share my notebook."

With only three chairs at the island, I got up and went into the living room for the fourth stool. It was a catch-all for my spare blankets and a jacket or two, but I simply set them on the ground to deal with later.

"Here you go." I put it right next to Dani, and once Ian took his seat and Dani's hand was in his, we were ready to dive in.

"You want to go first, Eliot?" I asked. "Since Dani and I were together for the last several hours we can go last."

Flipping his small book open, Eliot tossed it down on the island and readjusted himself on the stool so that Stella Luna wouldn't fall off his lap when he turned to face the three of us. "I did end up finally getting in touch with Mildred. She was actually very nice. I don't know what your experience was like with her, or if her tune has changed now that she has some help, but she gave me some information I think we should pay attention to." He ran his finger down the page then flipped it to the next one. "That car repair shop was definitely an issue. Per Mildred, June played the customer the entire time, continuously asking for more and more information, stating that they just needed 'one more thing' before she could sign the paperwork. And when she ultimately denied it, she did put *Karma* across the top instead of using the *Denied* stamp they have at the bank."

"Was June the only one who got to make that decision? Couldn't Mildred have taken the paperwork and made a different decision?" Dani asked.

Eliot shook his head. "No, he's a liability, and no one in town or out of town has wanted to be the one to sign a loan for him just in case anything went wrong again. His best bet was June because they'd had an affair years ago, but she was just getting her jollies out of stringing him along. She wasn't going to give him anything but grief."

"That confirms what I was told at the diner then. Okay." I flipped to the bank customer page in my notebook and made a check mark next to the repair shop. "What about the hairdresser?"

"That one Mildred signed herself. June didn't want another hairdresser in town because she didn't like the owner's attitude, but Mildred found nothing else that would have kept them from getting the loan. They were a good credit risk, so she signed that one herself." He flipped another page. "The massage place is still in the air. June denied it, but Mildred is looking into it. She's leaning toward saying yes because they meet the parameters the bank has set out, but she's a little nervous about it not being exactly what it says it is. She wants to trust the two sisters who are applying for the loan, but she's a little skeptical of the one and her honesty."

"Who is she skeptical of?"

"She wouldn't tell me. It's not her place to talk about the customers, was what she told me. I tried pressing her, but she was adamant that she would not divulge any more information. And that's all I've got. Besides our adventure at the storage unit today."

I wrote a few notes next to the different businesses and then turned to Ian. "Anything on your side before we get to ours? I know you didn't have an assignment, per se, but I also know you had said you'd be doing some listening around town and don't want to miss any new info if you have it."

Ian rubbed his hand down over his chin. "I don't have a lot but some of it might help. Dani told me about Lori Baker and that your dad said she's been missing since the murder. I did a little digging around the internet and managed to be in the same aisle of the grocery store with Fanny from the choir. She's a neighbor of mine. She pointed me in the right direction, and it turns out Lori went back to her maiden name and is now Lori Thomas. That's why you weren't seeing her on social media. Once I hit on that connection, I was able to find that she left for her daughter's house the day before the murder. She's a thousand miles away in Missouri right now, so I highly doubt she's the one we're looking for."

While I was glad to be crossing people off the list, I was a little nervous that none of this helped to clear Nancy as our culprit.

"Well, we have some info from Nancy and some more questions," I said, turning the page back to my full rundown. "We have the note on my car, the note on Nancy's car, the key to the storage, the note on the vanity, and not a lot of anything else."

"Well, we do have that guy who tried to shove a note under the door of the storage," Dani said. "You're still waiting to hear from Shelby about who she gave the master code to, so there's still hope."

"Of course there is, Dani," Eliot said as he put Stella back on the ground and rounded the island to open the oven. "We're not out of leads at all, and if we can figure out who the guy attached to Shelby is, we'll have a whole other avenue to go down." He gave the pot a quick stir. I was fascinated by the way his arm muscles bunched and flexed, so entranced that I almost missed my phone ringing in my pocket.

Dani giggled as she nudged me. "You might want to answer that."

"Oh, yeah, right." I could feel the blush creeping up from my neck and couldn't avoid seeing the small smile on Eliot's face. I accepted the call before I said anything I might regret. "Hello?"

"Hey, it's Seth. I was bored, so I watched the rest of that footage on the unit, and I think I found something you are most definitely going to want to hear about."

CHAPTER NINETEEN

"I'm here for it! Can I put you on speaker phone though? That way I can write stuff down, and I won't have to repeat myself? I have Dani, Ian, and Eliot here with me."

Stella Luna chose that moment to finally come over to me and meow into the phone right in my face.

"Sure." He waited a beat. "Is your cat Scooby Doo then?"

"Nicely done," I said then put the phone on the countertop and hit the speaker. "We're all here, even Scooby Stella."

"Ah, um, okay, so like I was saying at first, I got bored this afternoon, and I rewound the video to look from where you left off, Jax. That guy came through again an hour after you stopped the video, and this time, he had someone with him. Short, balding, paunch. The first guy was trying to hand the other guy a piece of paper and was waving it around. Looked like maybe he was yelling? Anyway, the shorter guy turned to the lock and opened it, threw the door up, and then shoved the guy in there. He was strong for being smaller. I couldn't see what happened from there but the short one did not follow the tall one in—he just waited outside. The tall one came back out, and they barely said two words before the tall guy left in his little compact car. The shorter one hung out for a minute or two, and then he left."

"Eliot here, Seth. Is there any chance at all that you'd have the ability to tell us who officially rents that storage? I'm sure there's some policy that makes that a shady thing to ask, but we really need to know."

We all heard clicking, and I so hoped he would share what he found when he found it.

"Huh."

"What's huh, Seth? Huh what?"

"Well, it looks like it belongs to Herbert Johnson. Dani, you're on here as someone who is allowed into the unit, but your mom's name is in the comments section in all caps and bold to never let in."

Dani's eyes widened. Time to disconnect before she said anything we didn't want to leave the room.

"Okay, Seth, thanks so much for the info."

"Sure thing. If I find anything else, I'll let you know." There was a ding in the background that sounded like the door to the office opening. He must have moved his mouth away from the phone because I heard his voice muffled as he greeted whoever had come in and then say, "Just a minute, babe."

"Let us know if you find anything else. We'll keep an eye on the phone. Appreciate your help." Eliot hit the disconnect button then flipped my phone over on the counter.

We all sat in silence, staring at my phone. I wasn't sure what to say first. There was a lot to unpack.

"Wow." Finally, Dani said something. It was like a dam broke.

"Why isn't your mom allowed in a unit that has all her stuff?" Ian asked.

"Do you think he's been hiding the things she threw away?" That was from Eliot.

"Why did he lie and say he didn't know anything about the storage unit when he's the one who rented it?" My question was last, but the one Dani responded to first.

"I don't know, but we're about to find out." She opened her phone and placed a call to Dad of My Heart, which was far different than the name she'd given her mom in her phone.

I sure hoped he had some really good reason for the secrecy and the lies.

She put it on speaker phone, and we all waited breathlessly for him to pick up. But he never did. Once the voicemail came on, Dani left a terse message asking him to call her and then hung up. Just as she hit the off button on her phone, though, a text came through from Herbert, telling her he was in the middle of dinner and that he'd call back later.

Which left us waiting. For Shelby, for Herbert, for any answers at all to make sense of what was going on.

"So what do we do now?" I asked. "We could keep going through the info, but I have this feeling that we could end up down some crazy rabbit hole that's going to be filled in behind us once we find out who the tall guy is and what Herbert is up to."

"Honestly, I think we should wait, Eliot said. "Having real answers from people instead of just working with gossip would be far better. In the meantime, we can feed ourselves until we're stuffed." As if to make Eliot's point, the timer went off on my oven, signaling that the bread was cool enough to now safely cut. Dinner was served.

I got out bowls and spoons and drinks, as well as my completely unused cutting board, where Eliot placed the still warm and absolutely delicious-smelling bread he'd had resting on the counter. I handed him a knife and he got to slicing.

"I have one very important question for you, Ian, and depending on how you answer it, you will be judged accordingly."

He turned his gaze to me, a serious look on his face.

"Seriously, this is critical," I said, then paused. "Are you okay with eating the ends of the bread loaf? Because I'm going to be honest here and tell you there is every possibility that I might stab your hand with a fork if you take the pieces in the middle. Those are my favorite, and I defend my right to eat them with a whole lot of vigor."

He looked a little stunned at first and then flashed that thousand-watt smile. "The ends are the best. No need to wield your wicked fork."

"Good answer." I smiled back. "Let's all dig into the magic Eliot has created, and then we'll talk. I have a feeling we have something here that we're just not putting together. Maybe, now that we're all caught up, we can figure it out if we have full bellies and focus."

"Good. Let's eat, and then we're on a mission," Dani said, dipping out a bowl of stew, taking a piece of bread near the end and then moving to the dining room table.

We all followed suit, and Stella Luna took up her perch in her cat tree off to the side of the dining room.

I hummed low on the very first bite and would have continued all the way through my big bowl of goodness if I didn't think I would embarrass myself. There had better be leftovers to stuff my freezer to bursting. Heck, they might not even make it long enough to need the freezer.

"And you're sure you don't want to come over to the diner side of life, Eliot?" I said between bites. "Because I would seriously consider staying open later and adding lunch to the menu at Sunny

Side Up if we could steal you from Hildy." She wouldn't be happy, but our customers would definitely be.

He sat back in his chair and laced his fingers together over his stomach. "I'm not going to answer that on the grounds that it could be used against me at some later date, no matter which answer I gave."

"Fair enough." I used one of my middle pieces of bread to sop up the remaining broth in my bowl. Should I go get seconds? No, that would be a bad idea—but in such a good way. However, everyone else pushed their bowls to the middle of the table, so I did too. Time to get down to the information we had and what we could do with it.

"All right, this letter Nancy got says the writer knows your mom was the one who stabbed June because she saw it happen and that if Nancy doesn't fall in line with whatever this person wants, they will get her. Whatever that means. But we have no idea what that even means, what line the person wants her in, or how the writer could have witnessed something that didn't happen," I said. I flipped my notebook open and then brought up the pictures I'd taken on my phone. I passed it to Eliot who looked it over then passed it to Ian.

Dani took a deep breath. "The problem is I don't know who to believe anymore."

Yikes.

"With the storage unit and Seth saying that Herbert is the renter and that my mom isn't allowed to enter—in bold letters. But we saw her enter and then come back out with nothing in her hands. I'm not sure what anything means anymore."

"There are a couple of different things that could be happening." Eliot held up a finger. "One, is it possible that your mom knows about the storage unit and the notice on her being banned was recently posted because she really does want to throw away everything now, and Herbert has been keeping her from doing that?" He held up another finger. "Two, was your mom not aware of it at all, thinking that anything she threw out was in the dump somewhere but instead Herbert has been taking all the things and putting them in a storage unit for you? Maybe she recently heard about it or found out about it and you saw her going to verify if it was true." One more finger up. "Three, well I'm not sure about three, but is it possible for you to make Herbert talk when he calls back?"

"It's possible, but I don't know if he'll answer me. He and my mom are a strange couple. I don't know why either of them stays, and it's not the kind of marriage I would ever want, but I have to think he has his reasons for staying, and I know she does because she doesn't want to be alone."

"It could be sort of like the kind of friendship she had with June all those years ago, staying with each other because it was them against the world even though, really, they're against each other too?"

"I have no idea." Dani shrugged. "They had arguments about me, and Herbert would always stay quiet when my mom yelled at him when I was younger. He'd often quietly go against whatever decision she made if it would affect me negatively, and he'd take the brunt of the fight once she found out what he'd done. I don't go around them much anymore, but I doubt that has changed. Any time I do see them, she's still the aggressor and he's the acquiescer. I text each of them separately, and I haven't spent any real time at the house in years and years."

"Can you text him now and ask him when he's going to be done with dinner? I think we might get the truer answers out of him." Nancy was at her salsa class, not to mention Dani would probably have a better time dealing with Herbert than her mom right now.

"Can do." She took her phone out and shot off the text, and then we moved on to the other pieces we had. Unfortunately, we didn't come up with much of anything that made sense. The choir was out, and the inheritance appeared to be settled and had no issues. Banking loan applicants could be angry about the decisions made about their loan requests, but was that enough to make a person kill?

Shelby never did call me back, so I placed another call as everyone was splitting up for the evening. I had to leave another message, but I put more urgency in this one. Tomorrow was another early day. Dani and Ian walked out together, and Eliot lingered in the kitchen, cleaning up and putting everything away.

"You made dinner, it should totally be my job to clean up. You don't have to do everything."

"I think better when my hands are busy."

"Then think away. I wish we had something concrete to go on. I'd really like to know who the guy at the storage unit was with the master code. I bet Shelby's not calling me back because my number is not in her phone and probably being labeled as spam."

"I'm assuming she lives in the area?" Eliot folded a new dishtowel over the handle of the oven and then leaned back against the appliance.

"She does. I hate to just show up on her doorstep, though. That would be creepier than a random phone call from someone you don't know."

"What about asking Seth to have the owner call her sister and get her to answer the phone?"

Now that I could do. Eliot kept puttering around my kitchen with his Stella Luna shadow as I waited for Seth to answer the phone. I looked at the clock and realized he was way past closed. I was about to hang up when he answered.

"Hey, Jax, sorry. I was in the middle of something. Did you get any answers?" I could hear something in the background but didn't ask what it was. I was already taking up his off time—I didn't need to take up more.

"Shelby hasn't called me back yet. I was wondering if you could maybe ask your boss to give her a heads up that I'm not some random spam caller wanting her to send me gift cards?"

"Yeah, of course." He said something else away from the phone, and I didn't pick it up, but I did hear a woman giggle, and then he came back to me. "I just sent her a text, and she texted right back that she's letting her know now. Give me a call if you get any new info, okay?"

"I don't want to interrupt you again."

"That's all right. I'm just hanging out with a friend. I don't mind, and she won't either."

I heard the giggle again, and the sound pinged in my brain. Suddenly, it registered that it had to be one of the gaggle of gigglers from the theater. But which one? And how could I ask without sounding strange?

I wrote my question down in my notebook and then turned the page to face Eliot. He read it and made a motion for me to keep Seth talking. While Eliot was thinking? For how long? This felt awkward already, and I wasn't sure how to keep him Seth on the phone since I just told him I didn't want to interrupt his time.

And then it hit me. "Oh, hey, I wanted to thank you again so much for all your help today and for watching more of the video. I should have stayed, but Dani needed some fresh air."

"No doubt," Seth answered. "I'm sure she's not exactly happy her mom is being looked at for murdering June and that her stepdad is hiding a storage unit."

"Right, I doubt she's happy." But did *he* sound happy? Dani had said that after she and Seth had dated a few times, he had been angry when she'd cut it off. Was that revenge tinting his voice? Or was I just suspecting everyone because I was looking for a killer?

"Yeah, Bianca was just telling me about the fight outside the theater before my aunt was killed. We live in crazy times when two older women are going after each other over Nancy thinking my aunt wanted anything to do with Dani's stepdad, Herbert. He's a nice guy, but Aunt June already had a nice guy. She didn't need another and certainly not one who was married to someone she already had issues with."

"Yeah, that's a mindbender." I felt a little like Dani at that table of choir members, agreeing just to be able to escape. Now that I had a name for which of the gaggle was with Seth, I didn't need to keep up the conversation. But how to end it so it felt natural?

Fortunately, my phone beeped with an incoming call. When I looked at the screen, it was the number I'd been trying to get ahold of Shelby at.

"Wow, looks like your boss works fast. Shelby's calling me. I'm going to grab the call."

"Good luck, and keep me in the loop," Seth said.

I didn't make any promises as I switched to the other call. "Shelby? Hi, sorry to bother you, but I have a question."

"Shoot, Jax. I apologize for not answering earlier or calling back, but I'm in the middle of renovating my rental and things have been crazy around here. I should have taken Margo up on her offer to put all the unattached pieces into a storage unit."

I tried to be patient as she told me more about what she was renovating and how long it had been. Cutting chatter off was not going to help me get the information I wanted, and it was really only about two minutes. I could endure that.

"I don't think you called so that you could listen to me vent about all my projects." She laughed. "What can I do for you?"

"Well. I was at your sister's storage earlier, and there was this guy that looked so familiar. Seth rewound the security tape for me after the guy left because I could have sworn he was related to my mom. Seth wasn't sure what his name was since he hadn't seen him before, and it turned out the guy had used the master code to get in. Margo seemed to think that you might have been the one to send him over to storage." It was the best I could do while not sounding threatening or like I was blaming anyone for anything.

"Oh yeah, that's Jonathan. I sent him over to get some paint supplies from Margo's pad. Are you related to him? How'd that go over at the family reunion since your dad was the one to put him in jail for arson all those years ago?"

CHAPTER TWENTY

I had no answer for her, so I stumbled through with a simple, "I must have mistaken him for someone else. Sorry. Thanks." And then I quickly hung up.

"Care to share?" Eliot walked around the island and hugged me.

I rested my head on his chest, one of my new favorite places to be, and sighed. "I'm not always good at the improv, but I guess I'm at least satisfied I got an answer. The guy in the video is the same guy that I've heard about at the diner. His name is Jonathan Stilton, and he got out of jail a few months ago after my dad caught him for arson. Isn't thirty years in jail a little long for that?"

"Wow, yeah, that normally carries a ten-year sentence unless someone died."

"Not from what I'd heard. I was told the property damage was pricey, but no one was hurt."

"Interesting."

There was that word again. But it triggered a thought. I stepped away from Eliot to grab my notebook. I flipped the pages back and forth until I landed on the business page. I stabbed a finger onto a line halfway down the page. "He was one of the loan applicants that June turned down! It was for a repair shop! That's what started the whole thing for him in the first place. He and his dad needed a loan extension years ago, and no one would give it to them. His dad died of a heart attack, and then Jonathan burned the whole place down and said the bank could try to get the insurance company to pay for all of it." Oh, that had some distinct possibilities for why he would have wanted to kill June.

"While I agree that he might want to take revenge on June, I don't know if it would be worth it. He's already been in jail, and I doubt he'd want to go back. Plus, I don't remember seeing him at the movies."

"But we didn't see everyone who was there. And maybe he snuck in the fire exit during the movie, killed her, and then left. Ian exited through the fire door when he left the theater after giving his statement. I'm pretty sure Jonathan could have done the same thing."

"Good point."

"I want to go right now and just knock on his door. We could come up with a cover story on our way…"

As he shook his head, I sighed. I knew it wasn't a good idea.

"I think that might need to wait until tomorrow afternoon." He pointed at the clock on the wall behind my head.

I closed my eyes and told myself to be patient. It was not easy. I wanted to do all the things right now. But it was almost ten, and I had to get up early. I bit my lip, my mind running through what we should do next, and coming up with nothing that challenged what he'd said. Dang it.

He tucked my hair behind my ear. "How about right after work tomorrow? Or since it's a weekday, if it's quieter than it was this weekend, maybe Dani would let you sneak out early to go do a visit. If you tell her we're doing something to clear her mom's name, she'd probably be okay with that, right?"

"You're right. You're right. I know you're right." I sighed and tipped my head up to look into his vibrant green eyes. "Why do you have to be right?"

He shrugged and kissed me. Fair enough.

The next day seemed to creep along as I served food to the much smaller crowd filling the booths at Sunny Side Up. I'd checked the Spy Spindle several times throughout the day and didn't see anything new and nothing about Jonathan.

I did see the giggling trio. Jess, Bianca, and Kimmie came in around eleven. They drank coffee and talked about any number of things including fashion, vacations, and Birdie.

I was wiping down the table next to them when Kimmie got up and carried their dishes to my bin right outside the door to the back.

"Kimmie, seriously, you don't have to do that. We've got this. I don't want you to hurt yourself." Or break any of my dishes. I reached out to take them from her.

"I'm perfectly balanced, honestly. It's no problem."

Sticking my hands behind my back, I just hoped for the best.

Once she had them settled in the bin, I tried to walk her back to her table.

"Hey, I meant to ask about our check?"

I stopped in my tracks then moved us over to the left so that a party of four could leave. "Was there an issue with the pricing?"

"No, but the back had something written about Nancy and if she was seen during the time June was in the theater with us."

"Oh, uh, weird. Do you still have the check?" My mind was racing with what could be on the back of the check and why their server would have written anything there and then handed it over to the table instead of sticking it on the Spy Spindle.

"Yeah, of course, we haven't paid yet, but we're leaving now if you want me to just drop it off with payment up front?"

"No, that's okay. You know what, breakfast is on me." I held my hand out, and she placed the check in my palm, face down so that I could see the words *Check with Petra about why Nancy was escorted out of the shop before they closed.*

That was not good…

"Interesting." I was starting to hate that word. "I'll check with Jennifer. She was your waitress, right?"

"Actually, it was Jacob who took the order, and I saw him say goodbye to everyone about fifteen minutes ago."

"Got it. And thanks. I'll handle it. I hope you enjoyed your breakfast." It felt empty, but I had to say something as my mind tried to process one more thing that pointed to Nancy.

"We always do, Jax." She smiled then went back to her table to tell her cousins that the food was on the house. The other two women waved and giggled, and then all three left without dropping a tip. Dang it.

They passed Eliot on their way out. He held the door for them, smiled as they walked by, then waved to me as he let the door swing shut. I lifted a finger, asking him to wait while I grabbed Dani from behind the counter and dragged her into the back.

I explained what had happened with Kimmie.

"Why would Jacob be taking their order?" she asked, checking the backside of the paper out.

"I don't know. More importantly, though, where did your mom go after her fight with June? Did she ever tell you?" Dani handed the note back, and I read it again. What had Nancy been doing? Was this why she had received the threat about getting back in line?

"You've been there for every conversation I've had with her since this happened. I haven't had a chance to ask again, and I'm pretty sure she still hasn't gone in to talk with your dad."

"Okay, can you maybe give her a call or a text?" I squinted with nervousness and looked away, knowing she wouldn't want to have to do that.

Sure enough, she sighed. "I'm the only one who can, aren't I? Okay, after we close. And speaking of after we close, are you leaving with Eliot? I saw him walk in, but he didn't sit down."

"Yeah." I took off my apron and grabbed my purse. "You don't mind closing by yourself?"

"It's not totally by myself, and we can handle it. I'll see you tonight, though, right? I want to know what happens, and hopefully, by then I'll be able to share what my mom has to say for herself and her time. Plus, I'm going to run Herbert down if I don't hear from him soon since he never responded after I texted him last night."

"Deal." I pulled her in for a quick hug then went out to snag Eliot by the elbow.

Once we were in his car, he leaned over the console and planted a wonderful kiss on me.

"I feel like I've been waiting all day for that," he said.

"I definitely waited all day for that, and it was worth every second." I adjusted the visor against the glare from across the street and buckled my seatbelt before I could try to get another one. "You want to grab some lunch and go see what kind of trouble we can get ourselves into?" I asked.

"You beat me to it." He smiled that half smile. It made my heart do a little skip in my chest. He was so dang cute, and sometimes I just wanted to cover his face with kisses.

I stopped myself daydreaming when Eliot cleared his throat.

"Not too much trouble." He cocked a brow at me.

"You sound just like my dad. Please don't tell me you think you can't get in just as much, if not more, trouble than I can. I don't have half your skills of digging into things."

"Right, and I'm not saying I don't trust you. I'm just aware of how you can manage to get into trouble without even trying, whereas I know where the lines are and how to keep inside the guardrails. And before you say anything else, let me remind you that you don't seem to always know where the guardrails are to begin with."

I couldn't argue, so I kissed him on the cheek and parted

from him with a smile that might make him wonder what I was up to. Let him wonder.

"Where to?" he asked, idling at the curb.

"I think I'd like to order takeout from Hildy and see if she has any info on Jonathan before we go to his house. I don't want to bother my mom again, and Hildy always seems to have all the dirt. I haven't talked to her much since June's death, so it might be time."

At first he groaned. "I eat there at least five days a week." But then his expression became thoughtful. "Except…"

"Except?" I had a feeling I knew what he was going to say because I had been ready to bring it up if he didn't.

"Except, I could get a good idea of what the new chef is doing without him knowing."

Bingo! "Precisely. And after we order, I'll go pick it up without you so that they don't know you are part of this at all."

"And it would also give you a chance to see if you can grab Hildy for a quick talk?"

"Well, there is that." I gave him a smile as he put the car into drive and released the brake.

I waited while he got to the end of the alley and stopped at the main road.

"Which way am I going?"

Part of me considered asking him to invite me to his house, but then I thought about my baby Stella Luna. She would love it if he sat on the couch and maybe got his scent on a blanket—then I could get my t-shirt back.

"Would you be okay with setting up camp at my house? I have things I'd like to go over with you, and I can order from there then head out to get the food. The timing should be pretty perfect."

"Do you mind if I stop by my house and get my computer?"

"Of course not."

And I'd get to see where he lived, which I was super excited about, probably more so than I should be.

I barely had time to be excited about it, though, since it was literally around the corner. "Wait, you live above the pizza shop?"

"There's nothing like being surrounded by food all the time. I'm surprised I want to be around it at all when I can smell it almost all the time, but this is my place, and I love it."

It was also where a friend of mine had lived when I was in elementary school. I'd loved playing in the stairwell going up to the apartment, especially because it smelled divine all the time.

I did not ask him to invite me up, and he didn't offer. That was fine. Again, I reminded myself we had literally known each other just shy of two weeks. It felt like far longer due to the intensity of what we'd been doing, the danger we'd been in a few times, but it was still short in my view of how long it took a real relationship to take root.

When he got back in the car, he looked at me and then leaned over to give me a kiss, and I threw all that logic and reasonableness right out the car window. I was aware, and reminded myself, that if I got too lost in the kiss, we were parked on the street, and the entire town could see us if they thought to look, which I was sure they would. I'd probably get a call from my mom about public displays of affection, but I threw that out the window too.

It didn't last more than a few seconds, but it felt a little like an eternity, and I was absolutely on board with that.

I subtly blew out a breath, I thought, when we parted. But he must have heard because he chuckled. He picked up my hand from my lap and then kissed my knuckles before turning back to the road and driving. But he didn't release my hand. He put it on his thigh, and I left it there for the short drive to my house.

As we exited the car and approached my house, we heard a commotion inside, but I wasn't worried about an intruder. I could very clearly see Stella Luna racing from window to window to peek out and keep track of our progress to the front door.

"She's probably going to be all over you when we get in there. I just want you to be ready. She hasn't left my shirt alone since I took it off to go to bed the other day. You hugged me and enough of your scent must have gotten on it that now she drags it with her from place to place to nest in it. She's obsessed." I didn't blame her.

"Well, that's… different." He chuckled. "I don't think I've ever had a female obsess over me."

No way was that true. I wasn't going to stand out here and school him, though. Not when Stella Luna had started yowling from inside and looked like she was doing her very best to shred my curtains in an effort to get outside.

"Brace yourself," I said.

He handed me the laptop he'd been carrying and his light jacket then stood to the left of me as I inserted the key into the door.

"So warned and braced."

My lovely cat did not disappoint as I opened the door. She

launched herself at him, and he caught her without a second's hesitation. Like before, she didn't make it as high as she was aiming because of how tall he was, but he bent to scoop her up and then let her climb his arm to drape herself around his neck as he entered the house.

"Fortunately, she's light," I said and set his things down on the dining room table. There were outlets on the wall and comfortable chairs where he could sit and do whatever research he wanted while I went to get our food.

We placed our order, and I changed out of my work clothes.

As soon as I was ready, I went back to the dining room where it looked like he had put together a command station with his laptop and file folders and notebook, along with a handful of pens.

"I'm heading out to the Poplarsville Inn then. You don't mind staying here?"

"As long as you don't mind me being here by myself, I'm good."

I shrugged. "Just don't look in the closet off the kitchen. You don't want to know what's in there."

"I already know what's in there, and that's why we're getting takeout from the Inn."

"Touché." I made the drive out to the Inn and rehearsed all the things I wanted to ask Hildy and how I wanted to ask them. I'd even remembered to grab my notebook to write down any information. I'll admit, it felt weird to have something bigger than the order pads I'd been using for pretty much everything.

As soon as I entered the foyer, Hildy grabbed me by the arm and dragged me back to her office. I was not expecting that and fought her at first just on principle. She shot me a look that immediately made me give up and just come along like a good little lamb.

"I have very little time, and since everyone and their mother is aware you're looking into things again, I made a list of everything you might ask and everything I know. I've also asked all the staff to keep an ear out for anything that might help with your investigation, and they gave me several leads. I was going to give them to your father, but since he has a bunch of other things going on, I feel you're a good surrogate at this point."

"Wow." She was not kidding. I had a sheaf of papers in my hand, a stack, if you will, and as I leafed through them, I saw she had highlighted certain things and used different colored pens to bring attention to words like inheritance, ex, choir, and enemies.

"I don't have anything more than that at the moment. If after you go through it all, and you have questions, shoot them to me, and I'll answer them. I promise. I want this answered and stopped, Jacklynn. Bad things are afoot, and we need to make sure nothing more happens. I do not like what's been going on around here lately."

"You're not alone in that thinking."

She nodded as she looked around her office. To see if she'd missed anything? She'd been in this space for more years than I'd been alive, and she'd built something here that I hoped to be able to build myself one day—a family, a home, an establishment where people felt special and left happy.

I stepped in for a quick hug. "Eliot is also eating with me, and he's going to be checking to see what the new chef does when he doesn't know who his customer is."

Hildy laughed, and I loved to hear the music of it, especially when so many things seemed so dark lately. "Fair enough, and good for him. I'll wait to hear what he has to say myself. This stays here, am I right?"

"Of course. I love you, Aunt Hildy, and we'll figure out what's going on and stop it. I don't want anyone else to be killed either. It's time to get to the bottom of this."

"You would have made a lovely detective, but the culinary world is very fortunate you chose to use your talents there instead."

"Like burning toast, and mixing up sugars, and spraying myself with the milkshake mixer?"

"When did that happen?" She shook her head and then took my hand in hers. "No matter how wonderful you are, you're going to make mistakes. As long as people can trust that your service and food are good, you can't go wrong. Besides, there's something to be said for having people come in just to see if they can catch whatever you're going to do that day."

"Nothing like putting me on high alert."

"Forewarned is forearmed."

"Truth." And that's what we needed going forward, to be forearmed instead of always reactive. Now if I could just figure out how we would explain why we were knocking on the door of a man I'd never met and one for whom my dad was integral in putting in jail for a whole lot of years.

CHAPTER TWENTY-ONE

When I walked back into my house, it was to find there was absolutely no room on my eight-person dining table and that Stella Luna did not in the least care that I had returned. Brat.

The light of Eliot's laptop reflected off glasses I'd never seen before, and let me assure you, he wore them very, very well. Goodness.

He must have had earbuds in because he was obviously talking to someone, and it wasn't Stella Luna.

"I can't access his record. Of course, but I'm wondering if there's a pattern here of some sort? It appears he's been in for far longer than his original sentence was set at. Is there a reason?" He hummed and made a few affirmative noises and then hit a button on his keyboard after thanking whoever had been on the line with him. Stella Luna had at some point chosen to sit in his lap instead of hanging around his shoulders. He stroked her as he made a flurry of notes on the pad next to his laptop.

"What was that all about?" I walked past him to the kitchen and deposited our food on the island since there was no room near him. We could eat in the living room if necessary. I had TV trays, and I wasn't afraid to use them.

"Something strange. I'm not sure what to make of it. I looked up Jonathan. His ten-year sentence grew to almost thirty before his release. Unfortunately, I had no way to access why that was. Except, I was able to get a hold of a buddy of mine just now and ask some questions. It seems every time he was almost ready to be released, he would do something that extended his time—he'd get into fights, smuggle something in and then not hide it well, incite a riot—something so that they had no choice but to give him more time. But he got out six months ago, and he still hasn't done anything wrong this time, so why now? And why had he been extending that prison time over and over?"

That last question sounded more like he was talking to himself, but I answered it anyway. "Maybe he was waiting for something and that something happened, so then he wanted to get out?" I started emptying the very fancy bags Hildy had put our food in and wondered if that was something we could do for the diner. Then I let the idea go. No one cared if their hash browns came in a regular plastic bag, and they certainly wouldn't want to pay more just so that I could tie a whimsical bow of satin around their creamed chipped beef.

"A definite possibility." He picked up his papers and tapped them into line on the table. He also organized the small piles of sticky notes, napkins, and notecards he had spread out.

Seriously, we needed to think more about how to get this all in one place so that we didn't miss anything. Everyone had their own notebook where they were collecting info, but I would have loved to have a posterboard where we could see the bigger picture in one snapshot instead of having to continuously flip pages back and forth. I'd say next time we'd do it differently, but I honestly hoped there would be no next time.

"That smells delicious." He rose from the table and brought Stella Luna with him as he came into the kitchen. I had everything on plates because this food was too expensive and too yummy-looking to eat out of Styrofoam cartons and with plastic forks. I even brought out the fancy linen napkins.

"I only have soda. I feel like we should have wine or something, but I don't have any on hand."

"Nah, I know some people feel like wine enhances the food, and I get that, but tonight I'm all about the soda. Bring on the non-alcoholic goodness."

He picked up his plate and went in to set his food on one of the TV trays I'd set up in the living room.

I followed along behind and got myself situated. "I have a stack of info we should at least collate. We have time before heading to Jonathan's, though. So, for now, let's just enjoy our food and have normal people talk. Tell me about something you've done recently that you've never done before."

"Dealt with a hotheaded but delightful and beautiful woman that makes me want to do things I shouldn't. She's also making me revisit things I thought I'd put away as not for me in this lifetime." He raised an eyebrow and a bite of a steak to his mouth. "You?"

In the end, Hildy's information was extensive, but it didn't shed any light on any one path in order to cross suspects off the list. There were people who had come in to celebrate that June was gone with drinks and dinner from three of the four categories.

The choir had ordered a round of her favorite drinks to toast her demise. I had never known a choir to be so vindictive and callous, but apparently, we grew them different out here or else something must have happened that was bigger than we were led to believe.

The ex hadn't come in, but that wasn't odd since Hildy said he'd never been there before. People had talked about his possible part in the death, but no one truly believed he would have cared enough to risk his new family and life. Plus, he was out of town on vacation, so he hadn't even been here to do the dirty deed. One crossed off the list, at least.

Other than that, we didn't come up with much during lunch. For his part, Eliot was impressed with his new chef and happy with the way things were prepared. I'd shoved food in my mouth after his return of my question and had hidden from even attempting to tell him what I had been doing lately that I hadn't done before. His answer had taken me off guard with how wonderful it was. Seriously. Cinnamon roll with glaze and maybe that white sugar icing. How could I not have feelings for this guy?

I hoped I wasn't kidding myself. What would happen if we were just living normal life? Would we still have the same connection without all this sleuthing?

Lunch finished, I quickly wrapped things up and opened the door to follow Eliot to his car. I must not have pulled it all the way closed behind me, because not thirty seconds later, Stella Luna shot out from the doorway, darted between my legs, and took a running leap at Eliot's car. I gasped as she sailed through the air, but Eliot rolled down the window fast enough that she went right into the car instead of smashing into the window as I had feared in that split second.

"You're going to have to bring her back in. She's not going to let me touch her now that she's with you." I would have sighed, but it wouldn't have done any good. At this point, I might want to just buy some clothes, ask Eliot to wear them, and then make her a basket filled with the essence of Eliot.

He left the car running as he cradled her and emerged.

Coming around the front end, he gently kept her in place even as she tried to climb up to his shoulders.

"It's like you're catnip or something."

"To be honest, I've never had any animal love being near me this much." Technically, I was an animal, and I liked being near him that much too, but I just kept that to myself.

"I'm not sure what to tell you. She's standoffish with almost everyone. She'll let my dad pet her and wants to sit on his lap, but after about three minutes, she is done. With you, it seems she just can't get enough." Smart cat…

"Will she stay if we put her back in the house?"

I wasn't entirely certain of that. As he approached the house, and I stood outside, she seemed to get the notion that she would be left behind and again started trying to scramble up his chest to reach his shoulders.

But he quietly talked to her, stroking a hand down her back. I could hear him tell her he'd be back soon and would spend some time with her when we were done with this errand.

Briefly, I considered that if Eliot ever moved in here, it might be a battle between my cat and me for who got the most of his time. I'd fight her for him.

Finally, she settled down enough to be left in the house without trying to escape again. She sat in the front window, watching us leave and opening her mouth wide in what was probably a series of irritated meows. My cat, the drama queen.

I put that aside for the moment since we were back in the car and on our way to Jonathan's house. He lived on the outskirts of town in a small cottage he'd rented from Mavis Firestone. I'd put a quick call in to her, and she'd said he was a good tenant. In her words, she'd taken a risk with him because he had made some bad decisions in his past, but she also believed that everyone deserved a second chance.

Had he ruined it all for himself by killing June for not approving his loan and stamping it with the word *Karma*? Obviously, I would have to come up with a delicate way to get that information when we talked to him, but that was the main question in my mind for our visit.

Taking Eliot with me was the best decision I could have made. He was someone who knew what he was talking about, how to talk about it, and then what to do with it in a way that would make sense. Me, not so much.

"All right, so here's what we know so far." I recapped what I'd found out from Hildy and what Eliot had learned from his research and talking with his friend just so that we were on the same page. It wasn't a lot, but it would have to be enough for us to at least approach Jonathan with some kind of idea about what to discuss. As a former convict, and being in a position of not getting his loan to re-open his car repair shop, what was he doing now? Beyond that, I wanted to know what he knew about the key to Herbert's storage unit. If he had anything else to share with us to hopefully help with the murder investigation, then I was there for that too.

Nervousness hit me as I walked up to his house. He lived in an older neighborhood. The houses had long ago been built for small families that had come into the area to help with working at the mills and booming industry plants that had gone quiet years ago, but the homes still stood. They were brick and square and well-maintained. His was beautifully manicured with lovely bushes trimmed into little circles. Mavis kept a nice property. Jonathan was fortunate to have been able to rent from her.

Something about the whole place gave me hope, and I wasn't sure why. Maybe because it was so tidy and homey. I knocked on the front door, wishing that feeling would stay after I came face to face with this stranger. Eliot stood behind me and to my left. I didn't drag him up next to me because I could do this.

I waited thirty seconds and then knocked again when no one answered. There were three cars in the driveway and two more at the curb right in front of his house. I could also hear people talking inside. Was he not going to answer the door?

Ten seconds later, after I knocked one more time, he finally did. Jonathan Stilton wasn't a big guy, but he was taller than me, although a lot of people were. His dark hair was thinning and his face, though lined, was not angry or even upset. He just looked curious to see two people that he didn't know standing on his stoop.

"Can I help you?" He stood in the doorway, his body filling the space so that I couldn't see behind him into the dimly lit interior. He didn't even open the screen door. It was possible this was not going to be a friendly visit. I just hoped he wouldn't slam the door in my face.

"Hi, Mr. Stilton. I found a key in a jukebox at my diner and was told you might have some information about what the key goes to."

"I don't know anything about any key." And then he did slam the door in my face. Excellent.

CHAPTER TWENTY-TWO

Well, *now* what was I going to do? I hadn't even had a chance to ask why he had been at the storage unit, not once but twice.

I turned to Eliot, who shrugged his wide shoulders. A fat lot of good he was at the moment. Though that wasn't fair. He'd been plenty of help in many ways, and he made it so I wasn't standing out here all by myself while I tried to figure out what to do next.

The door whipped back open and then seemed to stutter back and forth between almost open and nearly closed. What on earth was going on?

"Give me a second," Jonathan said with a sigh. He let go of the door, and it slammed again.

"Should we just leave?" I asked Eliot.

"No, he asked us to wait, so we'll wait. I have a feeling there's another feisty animal behind this newest issue."

When Jonathan opened the door again, it was with a small dog tucked under his arm like a football he was going to run down the field. The little menace opened and closed its mouth, but nothing came out.

"Sorry about that. I'm dog sitting, and he doesn't have a voice—something to do with what he endured before he was rescued. He gets antsy when the door is opened and will jump on it to shut it. I wasn't watching the first time, and he snuck up behind me to pounce on the door. What's this about a key?"

"We found a key at the diner, and it led us to a storage unit. The owner's sister said she sent you over to the storage facility to get some paint supplies, but you also stopped at another unit and tried to put something into it by slipping it under the door?"

I was taking a risk by giving that much of the story, but I hoped, if we could get him to trust us, that he'd either tell us why he was not the killer or give us clues on how he most definitely was.

Either I would take to my dad to verify.

Jonathan sighed and then opened the door wider so that he could reach the screen door latch. "You might as well come in for this. It's not the kind of conversation I'm willing to have on the front stoop."

Not wanting to make the wrong decision, I turned to Eliot to see what he thought. He nodded his head and then stepped in front of me to enter first. Totally fine by me.

When I walked in behind Eliot, I could see that there were two men in the living room behind Jonathan, younger men, maybe relatives? There was also a woman who looked to be about their age too. One man got up from the couch and came to stand behind Jonathan, similar to how Eliot had stood behind me.

Why did I feel like we were a breath away from a full-out confrontation when all I wanted to know about was the key and him being at a storage unit?

"Thanks for coming back to the door," I said.

"You need anything here, Jonathan, or can we go back out to the garage? I want to get under the hood of that thing before the deadline." This from the guy right behind him.

Jonathan hadn't put the dog down yet, so he turned with the small animal, and I could see the little tail wagging like a metronome set on high speed.

"Yeah, just be careful with it. The custom…the guy was hoping we could fix it without too much damage to the paint. You know what to do."

"We'll make it work." The second man pulled on the brim of his baseball cap and then left out the back door. Since this house was built along the lines of a shotgun house, I was able to see out into the backyard when the door was opened. I clutched the fabric at my thigh with my fist when I saw a cherry red car with a racing stripe. Wasn't that the kind of car someone had seen rush away from the movie theater after June had been killed?

I'd have to ask Eliot later. I desperately wished I could open up my notebook and verify, but here was not the place, and this was not the time.

"Why don't you come in and have a seat? Sorry about the mess. Otis just got here yesterday." He braced his hands around the little dog who had gone from tail wagging to full-body wagging.

"We don't want to take up too much of your time. What are

you working on out there?" Eliot said.

"Doing a favor for a friend's kid. Right now, I'm just trying to make enough to get by until I can hopefully re-open my shop. I have a few irons in the fire about that. Maybe one of them will pan out this time."

He took a seat in an armchair, which left the couch for Eliot and me. I scooted to the very edge and was ready to make a mad dash if anything went awry.

"So… the key?" Jonathan said.

How much should I say? I'd be cautious but not hold back too much. I was trusting Eliot to watch his reactions and read between the lines of what Jonathan said. He was far better at that than I was.

"Look, here's what we have seen, and if you can fill in any of the info gaps, we'd appreciate it." He nodded, so I continued. "The storage unit has you using the master code to get through the gate. Shelby said she sent you down there to get some paint because she's renovating. But I also know that you stopped at a storage unit and appeared to be trying to stuff something under the door. I just need to know if you succeeded."

"Stupidest damn thing I ever agreed to do if you ask me."

"We are asking you." Eliot leaned forward, resting his elbows on his knees. "I was a cop a while ago, Jonathan, and I know a survivor when I see one. Some guys get out and then go right back in because they don't know how to function in what's become the real world while they've existed in stasis. You're making strides. Because it's possible that storage unit is in some way attached to a recent murder, we just want to know if visiting that particular unit was a hiccup or something more."

That got a chuckle out of him, but it was incredibly derisive. "A hiccup? You don't get much of a chance to hiccup when you have the record I do." He dragged a hand down his face and let Otis down.

The dog hopped—yes, actually hopped, not ran—to Eliot and couldn't get his nose close enough to his pants. He sniffed and sniffed and sniffed.

"What is it with you and animals?" I looked at him out of the corner of my eye.

He shrugged.

"You got a cat? Otis is especially fond of cats from what I'm told."

"Should I pick him up?" Eliot asked.

"He'll settle right in if you let him have your lap, but that's up to you. He might look small, but he's a heavy little thing."

"Do I just reach down and grab him or does he jump up?"

"He doesn't know how to jump up on the furniture, and I promised I wouldn't show him how, so you can grab him once he stops wiggling." Jonathan smiled when Eliot bent to get his hands around the sausage-looking dog with the stubby tail.

I used the time to really look over Jonathan. He wasn't the best dressed or groomed guy I'd ever seen, but he was well put together and seemed like he really was trying to get stuff in order now that he was out of prison. Would he really jeopardize all that for a favor? Or even more, to commit murder?

Once Otis was curled up on Eliot's lap, we got back down to business.

"Jonathan, we've never met, and I don't know you, but I have questions."

"I'm not surprised that you followed so closely in your old man's steps. What's that about the apple not falling far from the tree?" He shook his head. "Doesn't matter. I know who you are, Jax. Unless, am I supposed to call you Jacklynn? I would be fine either way."

Was he really this polite, or was he playing us?

"Jax is fine. I only answer to one person who calls me Jacklynn."

"I'm guessing that's Hildy."

"You'd guess right." I tapped my finger on my thigh. "So you know all about me, but I don't know much about you. You said it was a bad favor. Can you tell us what the favor was and how it was so bad?"

He sighed and rubbed his hand over the top of his head. "That note and Herbert. Well, Herbert's a long past friend of mine before I got myself into so much trouble. We saw each other shortly after I served my sentence, and then he popped up here the other day wanting to know if I could help him out with a little something. He was adamant that it wasn't illegal if I could get a code to get in the facility. He didn't want to use his. Funny enough, I'm helping Shelby with the renovation as another avenue for money, and she needed paint. It seemed like the perfect time to try out what Herbert wanted. But when I got there, it was easy to tell I had no way of getting the note under the door."

"What did Herbert say when you told him that?" I hated even having to say Dani's stepdad's name because it made me afraid that we might have been looking at the wrong person in the right house. What if the killer was Herbert trying to blame it on Nancy? Had he finally reached a point where he was fed up with her attitude and the way she treated him and thought that putting her in jail might solve all his problems? It felt a little far-fetched, but I'd watched murder shows that were far more out there than that.

Jonathan huffed out a breath, this time shorter and harsher. "He asked to meet me at the storage and told me he'd let me in so that I could put the note up, but I didn't want to walk into anything I didn't have permission to be in. And he was being shady, so I wasn't going to trust that he wouldn't say I broke into his unit or something if things went sideways."

"Smart," Eliot said.

"I have my moments. Not many of them, but every once in a great while. I watched him put the note in the unit though, and it didn't make much sense to me. I left shortly after."

"Did he promise you something if you'd do this favor for him?"

"It seems foolish now," Jonathan said. "But he is a little more friendly than I thought a man should be with a woman who's no longer his wife, and he was pretty convinced he could get June to reverse that denial she marked as *Karma*. But then she died before she changed her mind, if she would have changed her mind at all. Now I have to go deal with Mildred, and we all know how that one is…"

"Yes. Yes, we do."

"I'm sorry I can't help you more. If you need anything else let me know. Now that Otis knows you, he'll be nosing the door open to get to you instead of bouncing it shut. Silly little dog. If I can get a steadier income, I might have to make him a foster failure." He smiled again, and it really did light up his whole face.

Otis knew he was being talked about, so he got off Eliot's lap and stood on the couch cushion with that wiggly backside.

"You gotta put him down. He won't do it himself."

As soon as his paws hit the floor, he was right over to Jonathan, who petted his head over and over.

My phone rang in my hand, and I let it go, shoving it under my thigh as I waited to see what Eliot would say or do. As soon as it went silent, it started up again with the ringing. I should have put it on silent before we came in.

Eliot stood, so I joined him. He stuck his hand out to Jonathan. "It was nice to meet you, Jonathan. If I can do anything to help you, let me know. I have some contacts around here, maybe not the level of Mildred, but I'd be happy to put in a good word for you if you need it."

"Thanks. I think I'm just going to do the side work for a little bit. I'm a financial risk—I get that. Burning everything to the ground just because things aren't working out for you sounded good at the time. I was young and dumb and going through some horrendous grief. But I've paid the price now, and I'd like to try again. We'll see if it's in the cards."

"Good luck, and thanks," I said as he held the door for us. "I doubt I can offer anything near what you make to fix cars, but if you'd like to add bussing to your side work, I could make sure we have some shifts for you until you get on your feet."

He tipped his head to me as he closed the door behind us. Both Eliot and I were quiet as we made our way back to his car. I had questions, but I didn't want to be within earshot of the subject, or his friends in the backyard, when I asked them.

My phone rang again just as we got in the car. Finally, I answered the call, keeping my eyes on Eliot, knowing we had a lot to discuss before figuring out our next step.

"What's up?" I said. I sounded tired even to myself.

"Can you please come back to the diner?" Dani said. "I have a lot to share, and I can't do all of this over the phone."

CHAPTER TWENTY-THREE

―――

"We'll be there soon." I put the phone back down in my lap. "Dani needs me at the diner. Can you come with, or do you need to head home?"

"I've got time. Should we call Ian in, just in case?" He turned at the next road and headed to the diner on Main Street.

"He might already be there. Let's check when we arrive. We can ask Dani what she wants if he's not."

Pulling into the back parking lot, we found that only Dani's car was there, and Dani was hanging out the back door.

"I hope you're not too full," Dani said as she let us go in front of her. Once inside the closed diner, I took a seat at the lunch counter. I used the buttons at the base of the jukebox to flip the pages back and forth, wishing whoever had left the key would have left something more to work with, something concrete that would have told us what the heck we were supposed to be looking for so that at least I would know when I found it. Instead, I was running around like a chicken with her head cut off but who did not yet know they were a goner. Although I did have a lot of good information. I just didn't know where it led.

There were many things that Dani liked to make at the grill, but some of them could be a little weird, so I was braced for whatever delicacy she might have been cooking up.

What I got was a pancake that looked like a bear's head with two big round ears, two blueberries for eyes, and a lovely and crispy piece of bacon for the smiling mouth. It was the first thing Jeb had taught us how to cook when we were teenagers and had told him of our dream to run the diner for him one day. He'd said if we could make these without having to pour it into a cookie cutter kind of form on the griddle, we would go far. We'd perfected the pour and the flip over the course of that summer and were very proud of ourselves for our dedication. When we showed Jeb on Labor Day weekend before we went back to school, he'd been baffled at how awesome the pancakes looked. We were baffled because that was what he'd told us to do! He'd blushed as he brought out his own bear head form from next to the grill and said that he'd never been able to make the pancake without it.

Dani and I had looked at each other, laughed, and then shared our pancake with Jeb.

And now there was a perfect bear in front of me, and the bacon was making me want to eat a whole pound of the stuff on my own.

Dani knew me well, though, so she brought out an additional full plate of the bacon and two more pancakes then sat next to me at the lunch counter. Eliot took up post on the other side of me, smiling over his own pancake.

"Nicely done," he said, using his fork to cut into one of the ears.

We had chocolate milk from the dairy down the street and didn't say anything as we ate and just soaked in the silence. There was plenty to talk about but not right now.

I finished off my last bite, smothered in butter and our homemade, local syrup. After wiping my mouth, I set my napkin on top of my empty plate and swiveled in my chair to face her. She did the same in tandem. I forgot for a moment that Eliot would be cut off but then remembered that he could see over my head and stayed were I was.

"Now that I am stuffed with all the goodness, what's going on?" I held up a hand. "Wait. First, thank you for the special meal and for knowing what I needed and when I needed it."

"Of course." She patted my hand. "And for the record, you do the same for me." She drew in a breath then let it out as she slumped in her seat. "It's been a busy day, and I have info, but I don't know what it does for us."

"Okay."

"My mom wasn't at home when I arrived. Herbert didn't seem to know where she was, but he did tell me some things when I pressed him about the storage unit." She twisted the napkin next to her on the counter, and I laid my hand over hers.

"Whatever it is, we can work it out." Unless she was about to tell me Herbert confessed to killing June. I stopped that train of thought because I wasn't going there until she told me what had happened. "Spill."

"He was in tears by the time I left, and I felt horrible." She turned her hand over to grip mine. "He was the one who put the key under the jukebox when he came in for breakfast that day. He wanted to lead us to the storage unit so that we'd find the note on the vanity. It was supposed to be a note slipped under the door, but he said that didn't work out."

That confirmed info for us, and I appreciated that. "Yeah, we talked with Jonathan earlier, and he couldn't get it to go under the door. He met with Herbert again because Herbert wanted him to put the note in the storage unit so that he could honestly say he hadn't done it if asked, but Jonathan wouldn't do it. He was afraid he'd get thrown back in jail for trespassing if someone looked at the storage footage."

"That's smart of him." She sighed. "Herbert also said he didn't know another way to get us to look at someone other than Nancy without blatantly being seen as trying to shift the focus away from her. He didn't want people to not believe him just because they're married. He thought the note would make it clear that it had to be someone else, because my mother has never needed a loan and she rarely, if ever, has actually learned a lesson."

"I mean, he wouldn't totally be wrong to think that anything he offered, that wasn't actual proof, might not be taken at face value because of his marriage to the suspect," I said.

Eliot got up from his seat next to me and started pacing. "He does have a point about his information not being as reliable, but why the storage unit?"

"He…" She trailed off and looked down at her lap. When she looked back up, there were tears brimming in her brown eyes. "He's been taking everything that she throws away that he thinks I might want and storing it so that I can have it when he passes. He's almost twenty years older than my mom, so he thought it was a good way to make it so that he doesn't have to pay more emotionally than he already does with Nancy, but I would get the things that I care about at some point after he dies."

"Wow, that's just sad. Why does he stay?" It had always baffled me.

"He doesn't really have anywhere else to go, and he doesn't want to start over again even if he did. She's normally not too bad to him on the daily he says. They've actually been getting along pretty well recently, until she caught him talking with June and assumed

June was trying to steal her husband like she did with the first one."

"Oh." That was a perfect motive for killing June. Something we did not have for any of the other people we'd been looking at.

"Yeah, if Nancy was that outraged about June, and if that was what they were fighting about, then it makes it even more possible that she is the murderer. He doesn't think so, but I just don't know who else would have the same kind of motive. And Nancy had the weapon and motive—maybe she made the opportunity?"

Eliot stopped between us, his feet shoulder width apart and his hands on his hips. "I suppose that's possible, but do you really think she would have gone through all of that when she didn't even know if Herbert was going to leave her? It seems extreme."

"Right, but she also yelled 'backstabber' at June while they were going about their slap fight. Maybe she decided to put action to words." Dani's head dropped again, and she stared at the floor. "I don't know what to believe anymore."

"We'll figure it out. I promise," Eliot said.

"What was that place we were told to ask about Nancy's alibi on the back of the diner check?" I asked. If she wouldn't tell us, maybe we would just have to go straight to the source. I wished I had the note with me, but I'd taken it home.

"Hmmm…" Dani glanced at the ceiling as if in deep thought.

Then it hit me. "Petra! We were supposed to ask Petra why Nancy was escorted out of the shop on the night of the murder!"

"Petra from Days Gone By?" Dani said. "Why would my mom have been there?"

"I don't know, but it's worth looking into. And we might still have time if we hustle."

We all loaded into Eliot's SUV and made the trip across town. I was so hopeful that we might be able to get the alibi that Nancy seemed to not want to divulge. It might not completely remove her as a suspect, but I was interested in anything that could get us moving forward on figuring out who killed June.

When we pulled up at Days Gone By, there was only one other car in the parking lot, and it was Petra's. We watched her walk past the front windows several times. She was talking on her phone and arranging the outdated furniture and vintage clothes as she wandered around the store.

I didn't want to sit in the car forever and have her decide to close early because of no customers coming in, so we got out and made our way to her front door.

She had moved into the back of the store, so we opened the door and waited near the checkout desk. I didn't want to interrupt her call, and we had some time. Plus, maybe she'd say something that would help. You just never knew.

"I'm not sure what you want me to do then. I can give them your alibi if you'd just let me tell them what happened." She waited a beat. "I am aware you're not supposed to be here ever again. Linda was very specific about you not being on the premises because of the shoplifting last time, so I'm not sure that I'll be able to get around saying that you snuck in, and once I found you, I let you stay instead of immediately ushering you out the door. I can confirm that I had to check your pockets and your purse on your way out the door. At least I'd be able to tell them your knife was still in there and that it didn't have any blood on it." She waited another beat. "It's the best I can do for you, Nancy."

This was both good and not good. Eliot cleared his throat loud enough for Petra to most likely hear him because she suddenly squeaked and hurriedly said goodbye.

She glided out to the front on six-inch heels with a sparkle in her eye and a kick in her step.

Until she saw who was waiting for her.

Her whole demeanor dropped along with her shoulders. "Were you in here for the whole conversation?" she asked.

"Enough of it," Dani said. "Now tell me exactly what happened."

Petra groaned and put her phone on the cash register. "My best friend told me I should have said something earlier, no matter what it would cost me."

"I'm not hearing an explanation for what you were saying to my mom," Dani said, placing her hands on the counter with her fingers splayed.

"Your mother was in here when she wasn't supposed to be. After I had to escort her out a few weeks ago, because she had tried to steal some jewelry, the owner had barred her from coming back. But Nancy snuck in that night, and I didn't want to have a confrontation, so I let her wander and then asked her to show me her pockets and purse before she left so that I could make sure she wasn't leaving with anything she hadn't bought. I can vouch for her during June's murder, but it will put me in a bad position, because I didn't immediately kick her out, and the owner was very clear about her orders. I felt bad for her after hearing about the fight with June from one of my friends who was at the theater, though, so I let her browse, thinking it wouldn't harm anyone really. But when news of the murder hit, I asked Nancy if she wanted me to vouch for her whereabouts, at least for some of the time when June had been killed, but she didn't want that. She's adamant that she doesn't need an alibi because no one believes she would have murdered anyone. Plus, you're going to find the real killer, so there's no need for her to defend herself." She had tears glistening in her eyes when she was done.

"Typical Nancy," I said out loud, instead of all the things that were running through my head. Mainly, that she should have said something much earlier than now.

Petra nodded. "I should probably go talk to your dad, shouldn't I? Jess told me I should have said something from the very beginning, but I didn't listen to her."

"Yes, you should talk to the police. The rest can be sorted out, but if you know for certain that Nancy was here during the time June was killed then it would really help the investigation." Not to mention it would let us off the hook of trying to prove her innocence. Though I still wanted to know who had done this.

"All right, let me get my coat."

We stayed up front while we waited, and I looked around at the store I barely ever came into. My style was pretty basic most days. I wore the same thing to work every day, black pants and one of our logo polos. When I went home, I leaned toward t-shirts and jeans or comfy pants. They had some pretty things on the racks, though. Maybe if Eliot and I started actually going out on dinner dates, instead of investigating over takeout, I would come by for something to add to my sparse closet. Maybe.

Petra came out of the back with not only her coat but also a big piece of folded cardboard under her arm. "I just need to put this into the recycling, and then we can go."

"Actually, do you mind if we take that with us?" I asked. I just had a great idea on how to pull all our big picture information onto one area, and that board would be perfect.

"Sure."

She handed it over, and I texted my dad to let him know she was heading over to the station. He texted back that he'd meet her there, and then we parted ways.

"I propose we call Ian now and meet back at my house," I said. "We can put a bunch of things up on this cardboard and see if anything shakes out now that we have one less suspect."

"I love it," Dani said then took out her phone and called Ian.

"Are you on board with that?" I asked Eliot.

"I see what you did there," he said and chuckled. "Yes, I'm onboard with the board."

* * *

An hour later, the four of us were back in the dining room. Stella had made her passes at Eliot but kept a farther distance after smelling dog on him. She'd get over it eventually, and in the meantime, that meant he could give his full attention to the board we were constructing with some thumbtacks and lots of tape and glue.

I had kind of been kidding when I said our little town seemed like Cabot Cove from the series *Murder, She Wrote*, but I felt like it was no longer a joke. What on earth was going on here? I would never say we were without issues, but seeing all these town grievances and with so many people up on one board, it felt like it was spinning a little too far out into chaos.

"We need to start being far more proactive about what is going on and who is involved. I'm tired of running around after everyone and not getting anywhere. Things are piling up, questions are completely unanswered, and I'm about to get testy." I stood in front of the huge board with my hands on my hips and an attitude in my voice.

Dani cracked a smile, like a real one, for the first time in a little while, and we looked at each other.

"Why did we think we could do this?" I asked her.

"If not us, then who? I know your dad is on the ground and is doing his best job, but you were right when you said we are uniquely positioned to be in the midst of a ton of information the police aren't going to hear unless they come down to the diner and drink milkshakes every day. Beyond that, people talk far more openly around us than they would a police officer, even if he is in plain clothes. Everyone knows everyone. Now let's use our freaking connections, get some answers, and start marking things off the list. I'm even fine with not knowing exactly who did it if we can hand your dad a smaller list than what would be in a phone book like they used to print. We have to dive in, Jax. If for nothing else than the fact that our town is being savaged, and I will not stand for it."

She hadn't mentioned her mom, of course, since we'd been able to put a big huge black line through her name on the suspects list.

Although we did still have that threatening note she'd gotten. As I used a thumbtack to put it up on the board next to the note I'd received in the grocery store parking lot and the random writing on the back of the giggling trio's check, I stepped back.

Now that they were next to each other, the writing on the two handwritten notes looked similar, but the threat to Nancy had been printed off a computer. So were there three different people all trying to warn and threaten?

"I really wish we could talk to your mom. She's no longer a suspect, but maybe she would have some insight into who would have done this and why was she at the storage unit that she had been marked off of? It might not lead directly to the killer, but at least that would be another thing marked off our list."

"I had a feeling you were going to say that, and I tried to call her, but her voicemail is full, and she's not picking up."

Eliot moved to stand near me at the board and looked it over. He touched the printed paper and then lifted the corner. To catch the light? To feel the texture?

"What did you find?"

"It looks like there's an impression of more writing here in the corner. Do you have a pencil?"

Of course I did!

Grabbing the pencil off the coffee table in the living room, I handed it to Eliot and then watched as he untacked the printed note from the board. He cleared a spot on the dining room table so that he could put the paper directly on that flat surface. We all stood hunched over the table in anticipation as he used the side of the pencil lead to gently scribble back and forth over the indentations on the edge of the paper.

And what to my wondering eyes should appear, but the exact wording on the note that had been left on my car, in the same handwriting! All three notes had been made by the same person. Perhaps the note on the back of the gigglers' check wasn't as random as I thought it had been...

None of the three women had shown up on any of our suspect lists other than being in the theater when the stabbing happened.

Although, what if that burst of laughter before the movie started, and then someone telling someone else to get back to their seat, was the murder happening right at that moment?

So many things to consider! But now that I could see proof that it was very possible one of them had been the person to warn me away at the grocery store when I was getting eggs, then threaten Nancy, followed closely by giving us a place to look for Nancy's alibi, it all felt even more jumbled in my head. Why? What was the purpose? There were several ways this could go, but I didn't have to figure it out for myself, since I was not exactly alone here.

"Brain check," I said and everyone focused on me. Now that I had their attention, I had to think about how I wanted to say this so it didn't come out as confused as it felt mentally. "We have three notes with three different intentions, right?"

"Yes." Dani answered first, so I focused on her. My partner in business and my life-long best friend could normally finish my sentences for me, so maybe she could help me think through this without messing it up.

"One note told me to stay out of things because nobody wanted me to get hurt. Another was a threat to Nancy to answer for her crimes. The last was on the back of a receipt at the diner even though no one on our staff had previously written on a customer's check. Everyone else used a blank and stuck it on the Spy Spindle."

"I'm following you," Eliot said, leaning back in his chair.

I smiled at him as the ideas were coalescing in my brain. "So maybe the warning one was to keep me out, but then when that didn't work this person threatened Nancy. But what if after threatening Nancy they found out that she had an alibi, and they couldn't take their note back, so they threw us a line on the alibi to divert us. Perhaps they thought once we were able to clear Nancy's name we would give up looking and just leave it to the police."

I hadn't been entirely sure why they would have given us Nancy's alibi on the back of her check to start with, but what I'd said off the top of my head made more sense than I would have originally given myself credit for.

Ian rose from his seat and went to the big board. "So, first we have a warning to you because whoever this is not only knew that you were in the theater on the night of the murder but assumed you would probably be looking into things since you did with the last murder." He tapped the note I'd taken from my car. "But if the writing is the same on the impression and the note, they would have had to write it assuming that they'd find your car somewhere and put it under your windshield wiper at that time. It was pure chance that you had to go to the grocery store that day. Right?"

"That makes sense." I wasn't sure where he was going with this, but I was here for it.

"Which then, once you didn't back off, and they saw you were not giving up, they thought to threaten Nancy to stay in her lane or there would be consequences."

"Right." Eliot joined him at the board. "The motivation there could have been to keep Nancy quiet from trying to defend herself. She has a history with a lot of people in the area and has been barred from places before, so maybe the writer thought it would be enough to cast shade on her and make her reluctant to defend herself, just in case something else could come to light."

"And if that came to light, and knowing Nancy and her attitude, they were banking on her being stubborn and obstinate. Maybe they knew she would have called her daughter to help but she wouldn't go to the police." I didn't join them at the board because there wasn't any room and I could do my talking from my seat.

"Are we thinking this is one of the trio who is always together?" Dani asked, and a light bulb went on in my head.

"Bianca was at Seth's after we found the message in the storage unit, so she would know about us looking there. Jess and Kimmie had known that we were using the Spy Spindle, and they were the ones who had the only check with information on the back. Jess was the one who told Petra about the fight before Nancy came in the store." They all seemed to have their hand in somewhere, but who was the person who had actually done the deed?

"All three have been in the diner together since the murder, even though they never really have come in before, at least not this much. They could be watching and listening to see what people know." Dani scribbled some words in her notebook. "Wasn't that the group of people who were giggling, and then we heard someone be told to sit back down in their seat right before the movie started?"

"Yes!" My voice rose with the word and made Stella Luna jump. "Whoever it was could have been up and murdering June then just sat through the movie knowing that there was a dead woman a few rows away. That's diabolical."

"Hold on," Eliot said and rummaged through his pile of

sticky notes and napkins covered in text. He crowed when he found what he was looking for. "I talked to Mildred again because I had a question about what it would take for her to sign off on Jonathan's loan. Since you all thought she liked me, I was prepared to test that theory. She wouldn't commit to that, but she did tell me the other loan for the massage place was presented by two younger women in town. A third was supposed to be on the loan too, but they took her off when they ran her credit score and she tanked the application."

"There are a lot of trios of young woman in this area. They like to hang in groups." I said the words, but I really wanted this to be right so I was playing devil's advocate.

"It might just be a coincidence, but if not then it adds just one more layer to the mystery."

"I'm with you," Dani said to Eliot, and Ian nodded.

"No need to gang up on me, guys. I was just trying to see any pitfalls before we settle on any accusations."

"Here's an idea," Eliot said. "I'm going to recommend that you take Kimmie up on her offer to help out at the diner, Jax. Out of the three, she seems to have had less interaction with anyone. Maybe we can narrow down which one is the murderer by having Kimmie around to see how she reacts to information coming through the diner. We have nothing to lose by testing out the theory at this point. We're not certain who murdered June, but if we can narrow our suspects down even further, then we might just be that much closer to solving this."

A man with a plan and one I could help execute. I was in.

Now we just had to catch her in a lie, and see if we couldn't turn that either into a confession or at least rule her out and then go after her cousins.

CHAPTER TWENTY-FOUR

―――――

The next morning, I was asking myself why I would even think such a dumb idea would work. Why think it, much less let it come out of my mouth? After Dani had left with Ian, I'd taken one more minute to myself before I'd jumped into action and called the lesser of our main suspects to see if she'd be okay with working the morning shift as a bus girl. She'd already proven herself to be adept at it, so why not see if she'd use the Spy Spindle again to try to lead us astray?

Kimmie was happy to fill in and almost giddy at the prospect of being able to clear tables and refill coffees as needed. I kept her away from serving food but did give her an order pad for her apron in case she came across anything she thought was worth jotting down. It was almost closing time, and I'd yet to come up with a way to confront her about possibly being the murderer.

We just needed one misstep. Out of the three, she seemed to be the one who topped my list to do that. She'd been in the theater and, just as the lights went down, one of the gigglers had told someone else to get back to their seat. She'd known about Nancy's knife, and she'd been a witness to the fight outside. Maybe she or one of her cousins had thought it was the perfect set up to use a knife to kill June and make sure that all signs pointed to Nancy as the killer.

I hadn't worked that one all the way out yet, but there was time. And we also had my dad on call in case Kim did anything she shouldn't. He was planning on calling her in this afternoon to interview her as a follow-up to her first statement. He hadn't been completely in agreement about not grabbing her right away and getting her to the station, but I'd convinced him that his case would be far more solid if I could catch her in the act of writing something so that he could compare it to the note left on my car, the note on the back of the check, and the impressions Eliot had been able to lightly tease out on the computer-printed paper.

We were only about an hour and a half from my dad coming to get her, when we were suddenly slammed again at one o'clock. The choir came in, some ladies from the bank, the ex-husband, and a table full of women who had found each other online to start a support group for those who June had decided were on her must-shoot-down-as-often-as-possible list. They called themselves the Juned Bugs, and though I knew I probably shouldn't, I did laugh with them when they explained it.

With everyone sitting at only four tables, we were running high. We served, and we moved along as best we could. The whole team pulled together to keep the plates moving, the drinks poured, and the checks placed upside down on the end of the table as soon as the last item was served so that we could close at two without seeming to cut anyone off or push them out the door. It was 2:10 when we waved the last set of people out the door, including Kimmie.

I was bummed that I hadn't been able to get her to do anything that would thrust her into the spotlight, but maybe my dad could do more in his official capacity. It was his job, after all. I should have just kept to my own job and not think I had any hope of actually catching a killer.

It was 2:45 by the time all the grills were off, and the dishwasher run. I let everyone out at 3:00 on the nose even though there were a few things left undone. It was our normal clock-out, and I wasn't going to keep them today when they'd busted tail to get everything done and everyone eating and talking happily. In the last hour there had been no real information shared that I knew of, and nothing new had made it onto the spindle. I was a little shocked that out of those four tables, filled with the people in the groups on my watch list, no one had said a word worth writing down, but there you had it.

I had been so sure we had just needed Kimmie to confess her horrendous deed or throw one of her cousins under the bus. I was thinking maybe I had been too quick to lay out that case without any truly incriminating evidence.

In the meantime, Eliot and I were heading back to Jonathan's to let him know that he was in the clear and see if there was anything we could do to help him.

As we took the last right turn before we'd get to his house, we held hands and became more solemn. This was fun right now, but there was still a lot to be settled. I wouldn't feel completely done until I heard that my dad had someone in custody, hopefully Kimmie, Jess, or Bianca, singing like the jailbird one of them should become.

When we pulled up at Jonathan's house, only the porch light was on, but the screen door appeared to have been yanked off its hinges, and just looking at the house gave me a bad feeling.

"Smoke!" Eliot said, yanking open his door and scrambling out. "Call 911 now, and don't come in."

I made the call as requested to report the issue and texted my dad at the same time. Did he have Kimmie yet?

Thirty seconds later, he parked right behind us, and the fire department showed up a minute after that.

There was chaos as they unloaded, which increased when Eliot crashed out of the front door carrying Jonathan in his arms. Otis was close behind and silently freaking out.

The ambulance was on scene, so Eliot deposited Jonathan for the paramedics to evaluate onto the bumper step at the back of the vehicle. He didn't look hurt, so maybe the fire was just an accident, and he'd forgotten to turn the oven off or something.

Although, he appeared to be crying, which turned into sobbing once the dog was placed in his arms and a blanket draped over his shoulders.

"I swear I had nothing to do with this. I would never have done this." The pain in his voice was palpable.

I pulled my dad to the side as Eliot went to speak to someone in the crowd. "Is someone else interrogating Kimmie?" I asked.

"No. She slipped by everything we had in place. I don't know how, but she's out here somewhere. And with the fire, and it being at Jonathan's, I thought maybe this could be where she's trying to distract us while she gets away."

That was not good. I glanced around but saw nothing out of the ordinary other than a bunch of people standing on the sidewalk, watching the flames being fought by the firefighters. I didn't see her in the crowd.

The firefighters kept at their job while my dad and I stood at the tail end of the ambulance. The entire back of the house appeared to be on fire, and a second set of trucks had just pulled in to join the first. No matter what they did, they kept having flareups. At least no one else was in the house, and they should be able to just do the work they needed to do now.

We were left in the driveway as Jonathan and his dog were scooted off to the hospital, and every firefighter did their damnedest to put out what looked like an inferno. The cops were talking to neighbors who'd come out to see what on earth was going on.

"So what now?" I asked my Dad who stood with me, watching the destruction.

Eliot strode up on the tail end of my question. "Now we see what we know, and what might have occurred here in order to make this all happen. I can tell you right now that this was not an accident. Do you remember a red sports car taking off when we were at the movie theater?"

"Yes, it had a racing stripe. It was at the back of Jonathan's property when we came here earlier. Someone was working on it."

"Well, that same car is missing. It's been around for the last few days, but no one seems to know who drives it, or who it belongs to. It tore off down the street right before the first smoke became visible in the house."

"Did they say the make or model of the car?" My dad already had his notepad out and pencil at the ready.

Eliot shook his head. "They don't remember. But they also admitted they wouldn't know a Mustang from a Corvette, so their information is not going to help too much on that front. But the car itself is conspicuous, so we might be able to find it by asking around town."

"Let me handle that," Dad said. He closed his notebook and tucked it into the breast pocket of his shirt. "I'll get one of the rookies on it, and we'll go from there." He turned to me. "I almost hate to ask, but what brought you all out here in the first place? I'm thankful you were here so that Jonathan and his dog made it out alive." He looked back over at the house. "I don't know if that old girl is going to make it, though. Might have been faulty wiring or something, but at the rate they're going, I don't know if there's going to be enough left of it to find out once the fire is finally extinguished."

"That's sad," I said. "Jonathan didn't do this, Dad. I know he didn't."

"I don't doubt it for a minute. But there's a possibility Kimmie did and then took off in the car just so that we'd be distracted."

My whole plan had fallen apart, and I felt horrible that not only was the house going to be a loss but that the potential killer was now out there, running for her life instead of sitting in a jail cell as she should have been.

I went back to Eliot's car and climbed in the passenger seat, resting my head back.

And that's when I felt a blade at my throat.

Oh my word!

"You're going to very quietly get in the driver's seat, and then you're going to tell everyone you got an alert that the diner has been broken into again and that you have to go check it out. Those darned kids trying to get likes and follows on social media."

I gulped and felt the knife press harder into my neck.

"Do not scream. Do not even flinch. And don't you dare beep that horn when you get over there. June was an accident. I was only trying to scare her into approving the loan for the three of us. She knew I was good for it. She just hated me. But then I stumbled, and the knife plunged into her back, and I couldn't do anything but go back to my seat and watch that movie while I knew she was back there dead."

So June had been dead the whole time. Maybe we hadn't heard her yelp because everyone was giggling and talking.

"But then I had two hours to come up with an idea that was inspired really by Nancy, with her 'sticker' in her purse and yelling backstabber. I even texted Nancy from June's phone to make it look like she was still alive when I was told to get back to my seat by Bianca during the advertisements. It was perfect. Including the notes I left. Why couldn't you just not look into things? Or why couldn't you have left it at the threat to Nancy I made on my computer? Dani hates her mom and would better off with her in prison. Heck, we'd probably all be better off with her in prison. But no. You had to keep going. Even when I left you that note on the check after I found out Nancy had a solid alibi. Jess is friends with Petra, and she'd heard that Nancy had an alibi. By that point I knew things weren't going to go the way I had wanted them to, so I at least wanted her to get in trouble for being in the store where she was barred. She's a horrible person and should be taken down. She freaking honks at me every time I'm jogging and nearly scares me to death. She totally could have killed June just for spite. So what if she hadn't? You and your dad could have made the case if you'd tried harder. I know it!"

I hadn't moved yet, but with the knife still at my neck, she jabbed me in my side with something else and told me to move. I slid across as best I could, hoping that I too wouldn't stumble and end up with a knife deep in my body as my father and boyfriend stood less than twenty feet away.

Why had I come back to the car? I would have been safer standing at the perimeter of the fire and seeing if I could roast a marshmallow.

She moved with me from the passenger's side to the driver's side. The keys were dangling in the ignition. I knew if I started the car and drove away, I might never make it back to kiss Eliot again or run the diner with Dani and watch her grow in her romance with the wonderful Ian. I wouldn't be able to bother my mother while she was reading or make my dad roll his eyes at me ever again. I couldn't burn toast or put the wrong white, grainy substance into the wrong shaker. Ever again.

So I settled into the driver's seat, turned the ignition on, and then I jerked up the lever on the side of the seat and slammed the seat back into Kimmie while also blowing the horn. The flesh at my neck stung, but I didn't feel like I was dying.

Kimmie, however, was moaning in the back of the car when my Dad and Eliot came rushing to the vehicle and yanked open the back door. Kimmie tumbled out onto the ground, sobbing and trying to say she wasn't the killer and they should look at anyone but her.

She'd have to tell me how that worked out for her through the metal bars of a prison...

And then I was in Eliot's arms. He pulled me gently out of his car and ran a tender finger along the cut in my neck. "It's not too deep but I would prefer if there was no cut at all." He used a gauze pad to clean the shallow wound—where had that come from? In his pocket again?

But it didn't matter, because we stood together with his arms around my waist as we watched my father protect Kimmie's head when he put her in the back of his patrol car. She was going away for a long time. I could feel it in my bones. It was over. Finally.

CHAPTER TWENTY-FIVE

The next day, I closed the diner to customers but got ready to open it up to family and friends. I wanted everyone under one roof and at one table. It felt important to do it here and now.

There were a couple of knocks on the front door by regulars, and after the third one, I handwrote a note that said *Family Dinner* and taped it to the locked door.

Once the grill was sizzling and the toaster plugged in, the coffee streaming and the milkshake machine flipped on and suited up with its metal cup, I went to the tables in the back of the restaurant to get everyone's order. If I wasn't mistaken, this was my last order pad, and I had not yet put in a new order for them.

There was banging at the front glass door. Eliot made a twirling motion in the air, and I turned to see that it was Hildy plastered against the door. Like I would keep her out. She'd been invited, but she was late, per usual.

I let her in and hugged her when I saw that she had a big grocery bag of order pads with her.

"We don't use these anymore because everyone is all about the handheld devices. I thought I'd bring them by as a congratulations for surviving again." She smiled and then leaned around me to wave to the table set up in the back.

She walked past the lunch counter and joined everyone in the back. They were all chattering as I locked the door again. My mom should be showing up at any minute, but I didn't want to leave the door unlocked in case someone who was not invited decided to invite themselves.

I was halfway down the aisle myself when there was another knock at the door, and this time it was my mom.

That was it. Our party of people who were important in my life was complete. There was not another person I was willing to let into the diner, and that was final.

I played general as I ordered Jeb to make pancakes and set my dad up at the toaster since he thought it was so easy. Thank goodness for all those eggs Jeb had brought us the other day. The special jam was brought out, and my mom oohed and ahhed over my syrup, which made me realize she hardly ever came in. We'd have to fix that. Maybe she could start a morning book club. I'd even do special seating for anyone who came in for it. It could be our launch of the side room as an event place if we ever got the thing cleaned out.

Jeb must have forgotten how to keep the sunny-side up eggs from sticking to the griddle because all of the sudden smoke was billowing out through the pass-through window and swearing had erupted from the kitchen, words I would never let anyone say in my kitchen. Words Jeb, who was saying them, would have fired someone over.

I ran to the back door to air the place out as Eliot took over in the kitchen.

All I knew was that I would never let Jeb live this down and neither would anyone else. I let them all razz him for a few minutes while they chowed down on biscuits and gravy, pancakes, eggs, bacon, sausage, toast, and creamed chipped beef. I poured coffee and provided creamer, then made my dad and Eliot each a milkshake. Once Ian saw them, he changed his mind from the chocolate milk he'd originally ordered and went for the double chocolate shake.

Finally, everyone had food in front of them, and I took the empty seat at the head of the table. I was almost positive my dad really should have been sitting here, but since he'd placed himself next to my mom down near the other end, I wasn't going to make him move.

"Thanks for coming in and eating all this free food," I said then took a sip of my own shake.

There was laughter at the table. My dad shot me a look laced with censure that should have been accompanied by an eye roll, but instead, he kept his gaze steady. I smiled then took another sip.

"In all seriousness, I appreciate everyone being here. Heck, I appreciate still being here myself."

My dad nodded and forked up more eggs. Ian and Eliot did too. It was like a race to see who could get them all done first.

I had a feeling we'd be adopting Ian too if he decided to stick around now that he and Dani were a thing. My parents needed to consider expanding their porch furniture by at least two more chairs.

All kidding aside, I really did hope he would choose to stick around, if for nothing else than Dani's sake.

Right now, we just needed time to be together. I sat down and looked out over the table, so happy to have this family with me.

The conversation was quick and flippant, but each of the people at the table caught me by myself throughout our two hours together and told me they were happy I had made it through another close call. Of course, that was also followed by an admonishment that I shouldn't have been that close to the call in the first place.

When Ian left, he happened to look at the handwritten family dinner note on the door and smiled. "Even though I'm not really a part, I appreciate you letting me tag along"

Dani was still gathering her things, so I stepped out the front door then closed it behind me so that Ian and I could talk without extra ears. "Please just be careful with her."

"Absolutely," he said.

I didn't get to say anything else because Eliot came around from the back of the diner and signaled for Ian to hop in. After Ian said a quick goodbye to me, he climbed into the SUV, and Eliot rolled down his window. I folded my arms on the sill and leaned in.

"I'll see you tomorrow?" I batted my eyelashes at him, and he kissed me to the point where I was thankful I had the windowsill to help me stay upright while my legs turned to jelly.

"Yes, I have to see my Stella Luna tomorrow." He gave me a cheeky smile. "She very nicely asked me to come over and bring a shirt for her to nest in."

"I'll need to eat dinner, so that might be a good time."

"Of course." He placed his hand on my cheek, and his fingers went into the hair at my neck. It was not a cold morning at all, and yet I shivered just a little.

"Tomorrow then."

"And probably the day after that too," he said. "Maybe one of these days you'll actually let me take you out a real date. Just you and me. Maybe some miniature golfing or something where the main purpose isn't to eat food or solve a murder."

I felt my chest heat up. "I'd like that."

"Me too."

I stepped away from the car but then remembered something. "We still need to figure out the original key. Dang it. I forgot to ask Jeb to look at the key. I hope he's still here."

Eliot kept me in place for one more quick but thorough kiss and then let me go to catch Jeb. I waved to the two guys as they left, figuring that I'd have a dreamy Dani to handle and take home.

"Show me that key," Jeb said before I could get all the way through the door. Thankfully, he hadn't left yet.

I produced it from my pocket, and he took it to run it between his fingers and then stared at it like it would start speaking to him and telling all its secrets if only he'd stay quiet long enough and listen hard enough.

"No, that's not going to fit what I thought it would. Dang it. Well, it was worth a thought." He gave both Dani and me a hug and then went out to his car. He waved as he drove by. "Feeding time for the alpacas," he said and chuckled. "Hopefully, I will survive."

"I'm glad we did this today," Dani said as I closed the door and locked it. My car was out back, so we could head out that way.

"Me too. I really like Ian."

"Me too. Do you think it will last?"

"Babe, you're totally worth it."

She gently nudged me with her shoulder. "And so is Eliot."

I smiled. "I think I'll keep him around for a while anyway."

"Good idea."

We hooked elbows and strolled out to my car, ready to head home and get back to normal life. I had Stella Luna to take care of, some divine stew to eat, and a book that was calling my name. I was ready to hang up my amateur sleuthing hat. At least for now.

ABOUT THE AUTHOR

Misty Simon always wanted to be a storyteller…preferably behind a Muppet. Animal was number one on her list, followed closely by Sherlock Hemlock. Since that dream didn't come true, she began writing stories to share her world with readers, one laugh at a time.

Touching people's hearts and funny bones are two of her favorite things, and she hopes everyone at least snickers in the right places when reading her books. She lives with her husband in Central Pennsylvania where she is hard at work on her next novel or three. She loves to hear from readers so drop her a line at misty@mistysimon.com.

Check out Misty Simon's books, including the Sunny Side Up Mysteries, here:
www.gemmahallidaypublishing.com/misty-simon

Printed in Great Britain
by Amazon